T0103797

Incubating in the Deep

Also by the Author

The Wrong Chase
(co authored)

For Young Adults:

The Adventure Of The Magic Eye

The Adventure Of The Disappearing Drums.

The Adventure Of The Bulging Buffaloes

The Adventure of the Dancing Ghosts

The Giggling Statue

Incubating in the Deep

LAXMI NATRAJ

PARTRIDGE

To order additional copies of this book, contact
Partridge India
000 800 10062 62
orders.india@partridgepublishing.com

www.partridgepublishing.com/india

Contents

Acknowledgment

This book is dedicated to my husband *R. Natrajan* who was always my inspiration, cheer leader, proof reader and my first fan for all my writings. I would like to thank my dear daughters *Archana Natraj* and *Jyothsana Ramnath* for all their help in research and editing, and for all the encouragement and support.

Chapter 1

A Secret Hospital

A six storied building near Panvel airport stood like a ghost in the shadows, mutely witnessing the top secret unfolding under its roof. It was well hidden from the highway, perfectly suited for such activity. Actually, it was to be built out as a five star hotel. The name board, "Hotel Avantika", still stood there, confirming it. But the board was now concealed under the black plastic sheets wrapped all around it.

For the past three months, some hush-hush events were underway, totally veiled and hidden from outside world. To begin with, the hotel was converted into a temporary hospital with utmost urgency. The patients were all moved in the middle of the night, shrouded in secrecy. The patients were surrounded by an air of mystery and all identities were kept hidden. The second floor of the hospital now accommodated 58 ladies, all in their last week of their pregnancy. In the third floor, the patients were 62 young girls. The fourth floor accommodated full-fledged operation rooms with state of the art facilities. The fifth floor was set up as a nursery with one hundred and thirty incubators, all of which were collected in less than two days from various top hospitals from India, kept ready and waiting.

But there were no families waiting with bated breaths for the newborns. In fact, a very eerie and tense atmosphere prevailed. All the patients in the hospital occupying the second floor and third floor were in a severe post trauma state of shock. They were all being treated by a group of special, famous and efficient doctors and nurses, summoned from all over India in a day's notice. The patients were all in very feeble present conditions. They were all suffering from extreme malnutrition, dehydration and stress. Excellent care was needed to save their lives, improve their physical health and help recover from deep seated mental shock. Nutritious food and medicines and round the clock observation were helping them recover their health. Most of them were on mild sedatives all the time.

Today after three months, a meeting of all doctors was called upon to discuss the progress of the health of the patients. Looking at the medical chart of the 62 ladies they all agreed that after the intensive, painstaking care and treatment, their health was satisfactory. Now they all could be released. The doctors instructed the nurses to prepare the patients for the next day session and also set up the conference room set for the lectures.

Who could have imagined that this huge black storm had been incubating and threatening to endanger a million people…all this unraveled from a common day-to-day road accident?

Chapter 2

The accident

Four months back

It was a usual maddening crowd of a Saturday evening. The Mumbai population had as usual poured out, flooding all the roads, every Saturday, as if it were the last day of the world. It was not any different today evening at the Dadar Kodak circle signal. The traffic was chock a block out on the road, with bumper to bumper cars, waiting, honking impatiently at the signal. The street side shoppers overflowed from the platform on to the streets. As the signal changed to green, the traffic started rushing down the road. A mass of humanity again started to bulge out on the platform, waiting for the signal to cross the road and the crowd began to grow every second.

Two young girls stood right at the front line of the waiting crowd, chatting and laughing. Behind them, stood a young mother holding her five year old son's hand. Her hand was holding him tightly, listening to his endless chattering, but her eyes were wandering restlessly, worried about getting late for his gymnastics class. For a second, her eyes fell on the two young girls waiting ahead of her in the crowd, almost resentful of their carefree life. Through the gap, she saw that one of the girl, much taller than the other, had her hand slung in a friendly embrace around the other girl's back. The fair hand had an unusual, sparkling, Topaz ring. This sparkling ring's beauty caught her attention, and she started at the ring, admiring it without blinking. Suddenly, this hand showed a jerky motion and vanished from her sight. There was a now a sudden shrill scream, followed by number of people shouting. The shocked lady, managed to peep over other's shoulders and found that the young girl, standing in the front line, had fallen headlong onto the busy crowded road, and was instantly crushed, by a speeding truck, everything happening, in a fraction of second.

There was huge hue and cry, and the truck stopped after a few meters. One other vehicle collided on the truck as others managed to brake their cars. Two Police men standing at the signal came running. The young mother looked around but the other girl with ringed finger, she had seen just a second before, was nowhere to be seen. She dragged her son and started walking away from the crowd, her heart pounded in deep pain and angst.

Next day the ACP, Milind Jadav of the crime branch, was reading the morning paper when his attention was caught by the news

> ### *A YOUNG LIFE CRUSHED*
> *Yesterday, around five thirty, a freak accident took place at the Kodak circle at Dadar. A crowd was waiting, at the signal, for crossing the road. A young girl identified as Ritu, aged twenty five, waiting in the front line, suddenly fell down, in front of a speeding heavy truck, and was crushed to death. The police could establish her identity, from the ID card in her purse. She was declared dead on admission to hospital.*

A constable brought his tea cup, and said, "Sir, this letter has come for you. It was found inside our complaint box" He handed over a slightly crumbled, old, brown cover. The word "Confidential" was written in red, above his name. Jadav kept his tea on the table, and half wondering at the origin of the letter, turned it all around. Complaint letters are just dropped in the box and no one bothers to put it in a cover. This one was not only in a cover, but had come in his name labeled confidential. He opened the cover carefully. There was a single note book paper, which had a scribbled note.

> ### *Dear Sir,*
> *You would have read in paper about the accident of a young girl at the main road crossing yesterday. But <u>it was not an accident</u>. I was standing just three feet away from this girl. There was another tall girl, standing near this victim, talking to this girl. Suddenly she pushed this girl, in front of the truck, without anyone noticing, and disappeared into the crowd. By chance I was appreciating*

*the ring on the hand of this tall girl, and hence happened
to notice her hand movement. I am an ordinary middle
class woman and do not have the courage to come out in
the open. But having seen a murder in this close vicinity I
think it is my duty to inform you about this. Rest is your
duty.*

Inspector Aravind Kote, who just walked in, looked at Jadav, staring at a
letter and said "What happened Sir? What is there in that letter?" Jadav silently
handed over the letter to Kote. As he finished reading Jadav said, "So what
do you say about this letter? Inspector Kote said "Sir, a common man will not
bother to go ahead and write an anonymous letter to police unless they have
some solid reason for that. This person seems to have one"

Jadav spread the sheet of the letter on his table and studied it carefully. It
was an ordinary paper taken from a school note book. The edges of the letter
showed a unruly, tear, as if the paper was ripped from the note book in a big
hurry. The handwriting was rather scribbled, showing the urgency with which
it was written.

Jadav said "Who so ever wrote this, is a mother, whose children are in
school. There is a ring of honesty in this letter. I think we should look into
this matter."

Inspector Kote said "Sir, about eight days back, there was an accident in the
news, and I remember what you said. You said that the young girls in Mumbai
are now a day not bothered about their life. Then if this accident is a cold
blooded, planned murder is it possible that the other one was also a murder?"
Jadav's eyes narrowed as he thought for a moment silently.

Then he said, "Kote, Pull up all the information available, about the so
called accidents, in the past three months. Get them to me as fast as you can"
Inspector Kote got up and putting on his cap and said "Yes Sir" and hurried
out of the room. Jadav once again stared at the letter.

Chapter 3

Ritu's Story

Five months back

Ritu was restlessly waiting at Dadar station platform number three, her eyes scanning the crowd for her dear friend. The 08.32 Andheri train came thundering in and slowed down. Normally this was the train she had to take to her office and surprisingly it was less crowded. But Ritu decided not to get in the train. As the train moved away, the indicator above changed, to show the next train's arrival time as 08.55 AM. Ritu looked around a little worried now and murmured to herself "Why has Meera not come till now? Generally every day she is here before me and complains that she has to wait for me." As she thought of her new friend her heart warmed up.. "What a nice girl" She thought, "So pretty and rich, but so down to earth and helpful. And she has become such a good friend in such a short time!"

She felt a hand on her shoulder and turning, her face surged with happiness as she saw her friend. "Meera I was waiting for such a long time. What happened to you?" she asked in a voice half worried. Meera smiled and said "I am sorry Ritu, I am a little late. You know what? Just as I was leaving that album director, Sami called me and guess what?"

Ritu's face was all red with excitement "You mean.," she said with uncertainty. "Yes, Ritu you have hit the big league. You are in, for his next album, he had promised me. Next week we are going for audition" Ritu held her friend's hand and said "Meera, I don't know how to thank you"

Meera said "Shut up, Ritu. You got the chance because you deserve it" Their train rolled in and they got into the crowded compartment. As usual, Ritu and Meera stood very near the door, giggled on with their meaningless conversation. As the train started moving Meera gave her the usual, Ritu's favorite imported almond chocolates. Ritu had a weakness for those decadent chocolates, and Meera brought those expensive chocolates every day, just for her. After five minutes, as the train was just stopping in the third station, Ritu suddenly felt a gripping pain in her stomach. The pain was rising in severe spasms, and she collapsed in pain. Meera tried her best to comfort her. All the ladies standing around looked on not knowing how to help her. Meera said "Ritu we will get down in the next station and go to a doctor" Ritu nodded unable to talk as more and more pangs of pain, rose from deep down her stomach

They got down in the next station and with the help of Meera she managed to walk. They got into a rickshaw and Meera gave an address to the driver. She held Ritu close to her and said, "Luckily my aunt stays here, close by. She is a doctor. We will see her now"

There was no crowd in the nursing home. The lady Doctor gave her an injection and her pain slowly started subsiding. Then the doctor started examining her asking some questions in between. Finishing her examination the doctor said "Meera, your friend Ritu seems to have some serious problem. Let me take a scan to be sure". Ritu was too weak to think or protest. She was taken to a scanning room.

After twenty minutes the doctor called both friends inside and said "I am sorry Ritu. There seems to be some problem with your uterus. There are few cysts in your uterus. Mostly these are harmless. But since you have got serious cramps, we have to worry about them. I will prescribe some tablets. You should become all right in a week or so. Please come again for follow up after two weeks." She smiled and started writing the prescription. The girls thanked her and came out.

Meera took the medical slip. Ritu waited in the auto when Meera stopped in a shop on the way and brought the medicines. Meera brought Ritu back to her paying guest apartment and handed over the medicines.

Ritu feebly said "Meera, the bill for doctor and medicines? You have paid for all. So I would ….." Meera glared at Ritu and chided "Stupid. You call me your friend and ask me for the bill?"

Ritu smiled weakly. Sleep was overpowering her because of the injection. As she was falling asleep, a question came in her mind "Why did Meera take me to a gynecologist, for my stomachache and not a general physician?" She fell asleep before she could think any more.

Chapter 4

In search of truth

It was four days, since they heard about the death of Ritu. As Jadav was busy, with some other case, he could not get any time to look into this case. Inspector Kote who had collected all the information available on the four accidents, was waiting, but only today he could put them up in front of Jadav. The names of the four victims who had died in accidents were Ritu, Bindu, Jessica and Shilpa. All of them had died in some strange freak accidents. All the accidents had happened between Dadar and Andheri and in the most crowded areas. They were all young girls in their early twenties. Ritu was knocked off by a lorry, Jessica fell off from the window of her apartment, Bindu fell off from the running train and Shilpa had fallen off the stair case and died.

Jadav quickly read the reports, and looked up at Kote, with a shocked expression. He blurted "Kote so surprising! So far no one had ever noticed that all these accidents happening, over the past three months, one after other, and that too, all the victims were young girls?"

Kote said "Sir, this town is bursting with population, and all police persons are already over worked! That might be the reason, that no one had the time to look into the similarity in these accidents."

Jadav said "Kote, the common man every day read newspapers. What about them? Won't they notice something strange?"

Kote said with a sigh, "Public have a very short memory, Sir"

Jadav got up, and picked up his cap. He said "Come Inspector Kote. Let us start the case investigation, right from the beginning, but this time on our own way" Without asking any questions, Kote followed his boss.

Inspector Kote parked the police car in front of the dingy mortuary building, and both got out. Jadav gazed at the old shabby building and mused that this is the one place where people would never like to go even after death. The place itself was dull, cold, and looked eerie. A small group of three or four persons were waiting there, to collect their dead. There was a disturbing silence all around. Jadav looked at those family members who had to do this painful duty. Death itself might not be as painful as that of this collecting the body which was dissected, cut part by part and examined, stitched back, and bundled into a human form. Jadav looked around with a vacant look, while Inspector Kote found out the admin office. They walked towards the office building silently. Looking at the uniform the clerk on duty got up immediately and after a brief talk went inside to find the doctor. Soon a doctor came out. Police uniform was a part of his profession, but visit of an ACP, brought a bit of surprise on his face.

He said "Please be seated Sir. I am Dr. Amit Salunke, and I am in charge of the post-mortem here. What can I do for you Sir?"

Jadav pulled a chair, and as he sat down, he noticed the strong mucky smell which seemed to be permanently pervading the air there. He said "Doctor, we are looking for a particular doctor who had done the post-mortem of these four girls, who died in different accidents in the past four months "He showed a paper, where the name of four girls- Ritu, Bindu, Jessica, and Shilpa were written.

The doctor looked at the names in the paper and thought for a moment, and said "Yes these four accidents had happened in the last four months. Ritu's post- mortem was done just two days ago. I took charge here, four months back and hence all this girl's post-mortem was done by me. But Sir, if you don't mind and please don't get me wrong. Is there any new information, or some complaint about these girls? I am asking this because the police had already taken the reports of the post-mortem and closed all these cases as accidents"

Jadav said "We have received some information from our sources, that at least one or two of these cases are not accidents, but suspected murder. So, we have started our investigation once again" The doctor looked a bit shocked. He said "Sir I would show you all the post- mortem reports. See, if you can get any information, from them" He got up and walked back to his office safe. He opened it, and skimmed through the folders. Finally he pulled out four *folders*, one by one, and brought them all to the table.

Jadav had not really hoped to see anything unusual in the reports and he was right. There was no food poisoning, no external force or injury except which were caused by their accidents. There was no other hard-hitting factor. In all the cases, the case of accident was a glaring truth.

He pushed the folders towards Kote and said "Note down the addresses of office, home town, and an any information about the parents of these victims" He then turned to the doctor again and said "By any chance, do you remember, who collected the bodies of these four girls Doctor?"

Doctor said, "In all these cases, the body was taken away by the relatives who all came from different villages. In two cases both the parents were there and in one case a brother and mother took the body. In the last case an old uncle took charge of the body"

Jadav said "Did the relatives or the parents, enter their addresses in our records, when they collected the bodies?" As the doctor nodded affirmatively he turned and said, "Kote, You note down those addresses of the relatives also" Facing the Doctor he said "Mr. Salunke, by any chance, did you notice anything unusual in any one of these cases? Or did you notice anything strange, but common, in all these cases?"

The young Doctor was silent for some time thinking. Then he said with a bit of hesitation, "Well, Sir, I don't know whether this is of any great importance! In all these cases, the girls were very modern looking. I mean their dress, etc. All of them were, living alone in Mumbai. But their guardians looked as though they belonged to a very rural background very poor, and all of them were illiterate. In the present day, even the help, or maids, we have in our house, have a basic skill of writing and reading. So I was a bit surprised, at their raw illiteracy! None of them could write, or sign their names. They put their thumb impression, on our register. They could only tell orally, their house addresses, and our police men, noted it in the register. As these girls all looked so sophisticated, it struck me very strange, when the third case came in."

Jadav said, "Please tell me, anything else, you noticed about the girls. Say anything unusual, during the autopsy?" Doctor thought again and said "Yes, all these girls were looking a bit bulky on the overweight side. As now a day almost all modern, unmarried, young girls, maintain themselves so slim, this again struck me, a little odd"

Jadav said "Do you mean their body types were bulky?" Doctor said "No, they were looking like- you know what - they had just put on lot of excess weight recently, may be due to over eating, or due to, some tablets or pills etc, something, like that and ……." He dragged his sentence without completing.

Jadav looked up sharply "And what doctor? What? Please tell me anything, you observed, even if it looks, insignificant to you!"

Doctor said "Well, I happened to see a bit odd point, especially in the case of Shilpa and Jessica. The uterus showed some raw large scars. In the other two cases also the uterus showed heavy reddishness and swelling. But I did not go into a deep investigation nor did I write it, in my report. Since they were unmarried girls and were dead already... I did not want the parents to know about that"

Jadav said "According to you, what could be the cause for the presence of scars? Does the scar represent anything special?"

Doctor said "I am not sure, possibly, that it might be a recent abortion and D &C done or some treatment, for removal of a cluster of cyst or fibroids from the uterus, or any other treatment carried on for that!. It could be anything. But it struck me as strange when the fourth case also showed, the same signs. How could all these four girls all so young and unmarried died in accident one after other and had similar uterus problems? Since I am not a specialist, I cannot say anything with surety, but there is something really strange in their death!"

Jadav sat silently for some time, blankly staring at the files. Then he got up, thanked the doctor and walked back to their car.

Chapter 5

The next victim

Shredha was a little breathless as she climbed the staircase to her office. Her office was in the first floor and earlier she had never felt like this. She kept her hand bag on her table, and went to the wash room. There was a sudden pang of giddiness, and she held the wall for support. She decided that she should ask the doctor next time. This giddiness seems to be happening too often.

As she washed her face she looked at herself in the mirror. Of late she had put on lot of weight. Meera had told her that the medicines she was taking could make her a little fat. The very thought of Meera brought a glow of warmth in her heart. "Oh, What a nice girl" Shredha thought in her heart. "She is so good, to take me to a doctor, when I was in pain and to go out of her way to buy me medicines, for the treatment. Who cares like this now a days?' Panting slightly she walked back to her desk.

She thought about what Meera had told her the other day. Finally her dream was going to come true. She came to Mumbai only with a dream of becoming a singer. Everyone in Pune said that her voice was too good and she should try her luck in Mumbai. But one month of going from door to door to all producers she knew one thing.. Nothing works in glamour world, without some God figure!! Luckily, she could pick up a job at a call centre and she managed to survive. It was at this time that she met her god sent angel, tall, fair and pretty Meera in the railway platform two weeks ago. They became very close, and now they always travelled together, in the morning. Her new best friend Meera, had promised, to get her a chance to sing as a play back singer through her uncle, who was in the film line.

Two days later, a very weak Shredha, slowly got out of the auto just in front of the nursing home. Meera had to help her to get down. Shredha was unstable on her feet and was panting heavily. For past one week she had taken medical leave from office, unable to manage her breathlessness. Yesterday Meera dropped in and seeing her condition said that she would take her to the doctor. The same doctor, who had treated her earlier for the stomach ache, examined her now. She said "The cyst had shrunk into a very tiny one. But as you are finding it difficult to take the medicine, I have to perform minor surgery with local anesthesia. You won't have any problem there afterwards" Shredha was taken to the operation table. After half an hour Meera helped her to get out of the bed. Doctor said "Now since the operation is over you need not take any more medicines. Just take some vitamins to improve your health. I will write the prescription for that"

Meera made her sit in a comfortable chair, in the visiting room, and said "You wait here Shredha, just for one minute. I will see the doctor and come" As Shredha leaned back and closed her eyes heart in heart she was thankful to Meera. She thought that if not for Meera, she wouldn't even know that she had a gynecological problem. How wonderful that Meera had helped her not only with the treatment but paid for her medicine and everything!! Inside the operation theatre Meera whispered, to the doctor

"Is everything over, doctor?"

Doctor smiled and said "Perfectly done. You are doing a perfect job! Now we don't need this girl anymore"

Meera smiled in satisfaction, and said "Ok boss. I will take care of that part as usual" She walked out and flashed a smile at the unsuspecting Shredha and said "Fine Shredha let us go" They went out to call an auto.

Chapter 6

A search in the office

Jadav looked at the e mail messages received, from different police stations, from all over Maharashtra. It was so frustrating! All the four of the home addresses, given by the guardians, who had collected the bodies, proved to be fake, non existing destinations! Jadav eyes, flashed in rage, as he looked at Kote and burst out with a fuming anger

"It means that the bodies of the dead girls were not collected by their real parents, but by some paid criminals. It totally baffles me Kote, that why should anyone after murdering, bother to collect the dead bodies of he victims and cremate them? If they were not the real relatives, then, what happened to the real relatives? Who are they and where are they? And why not a single one of them had not even filed a missing report in any one of the police station so far? Why Kote?"

Kote said in a soft hesitant voice "Sir, It is possible that even now the real parents might not be aware that their daughters are dead and gone... Hence they had not filed any complaint" Jadav said "Kote I think this case is much more serious than what we thought of. It is not a case of simple murders! Girls are being murdered. Their bodies are promptly collected, by fake relations. They are all illiterate, or pretend to be illiterate, from rustic background. All of them are actually fake people, collecting bodies, claiming as parents, and giving fake addresses. This means so many people are involved in this operation. But the question is why? What is motive for murder? Then latter all this elaborate cover up done? What is going on in the background? Everything is so vague and blurred that we are not able to put our fingers on it till now?

Kote said "Sir, all these girls, were from ordinary low income group women. So the case of murder for property, etc is ruled out! The post-mortem did not show any loss of organ. No organ can be removed, after three days in morgue! Hence it is not an organ theft. So what could be the motive for these murders Sir?'

Jadav said "Let us go to the corresponding offices of these victims where these girls worked and find out if something is available there. The local police had already done their round. But let us see if we can get something which they had missed"

Jadav and Kote entered the office of the "Super Travel Agents" where Ritu was working before her accident. At the sight of the Khaki uniform, the reception girl's face turned white and she immediately scrambled inside, to call her boss. Mr. Bakshi, the boss came out immediately, and invited the officers to his cabin. After comfortably seating himself Jadav said "We are making some enquires in a case. In that connection, we want to know something about Ritu, your ex-employee"

Mr. Bakshi said "Poor girl Sir! She was such a hard working girl. Actually she came to this city of dreams to join the glamour world. Every day, she used to try, some advertisement or other. It is a pity that her end, came in this manner"

Jadav said, "Mr.Bakshi I would like to see the table where Ritu worked – you know the drawers and its contents etc"

Mr. Bakshi said, "Sir, after her cremation the very next day her parents came to the office. They wanted to collect, all the things left by their daughter as a token of her memory. You know

Sir, they even collected the scrap pad, used by her. It was such a painful sight. They were crying so agonizingly looking at each piece of stationery!"

Jadav exchanged glances with Kote whose face showed a total disappointment. Then he said "Could you tell me, who was the close friend of Ritu in the office? I would like to talk to her"

Mr.Bakshi said "One minute" He picked up the phone and talked to his receptionist. He listened and said "Ok. Then, send Maya inside".

Maya was a young girl, just around twenty. She entered hesitantly, and turned ash white, at the sight of uniforms. Fear was written, all over her face. Jadav flashed one of his very rare smile at her and softening his voice said, "Maya don't be nervous. We have to know something about Ritu. She was your good friend, I understand. Can you tell us about her family and friends? Had she talked to you any time about a friend, a friend who is very tall?"

Maya swallowed hard and said "Sir, Ritu has not talked about her family any time. I don't know about any of her tall friends. But many times Ritu used to talk about a nice friend named Meera. She used to say that Meera helped her a lot and was even trying for a role for her in a TV serial"

15

Jadav said "Have you seen Meera any time? Do you have any address of her?' Maya shook her head vigorously and said "No Sir, I had not seen her anytime" Jadav and Kote got up. Thanking Mr.Bakshi and Maya they walked out. One by one, they visited the offices of Jessica, Bindu, and Shilpa but the result was nearly the same. Everywhere, someone had already spotlessly cleared the office of every scratch of evidence!. Jessica was working of and on with some TV unit. But nothing was available there. Jadav said "Kote, I think these killers are too smart. If my guess is correct, at this very moment, they may be targeting, some other young girl. What a pity, we know that they are there out in the crowd, but we are not able to do anything!!" He stood on the footpath facing, Shilpa's office, with his hands in his pocket and a vacant look in his eyes watching the crowd crossing at the signal. The tall girl Meera carrying handful of medicines in her handbag crossed the road, right in front of them! Kote's eyes spotted her and he burst out in an urgency "Sir Look there Sir! Look at that girl. She is a little too tall for Indian standard and her face shows a foreign origin," Jadav quickly spun around, and said "Where? Whom are you talking about" But before he turned the girl had quickly disappeared in the crowd. The traffic signal now changed and cars and buses started rushing through the road, completely hiding the opposite side from their vision. And in another end of the road the poor unsuspecting Shredha was waiting for her friend to bring her medicine.

Chapter 7

A drive to the village

"Sir, at last!!" Inspector Kote squealed, his voice reflecting a schoolboy's excitement. "Sir, we have got a lead." In a small village Pugudi, near Alibaug, one parent has recorded a case of their missing daughter, Jamuna. This may lead us to something" Jadav looked at the print out copy of the email and rolled his eyes heavenward "Hope we get something here"

Three days ago when they found out that the addresses, given in the hospital were all fake, they had sent a network of messages to all the nearby villages to see if any parents have recorded any complaint about their missing daughters. And today, they had got one. Without wasting time, they got into their police car and Kote drove in frenzy, hoping to find a key to this mystery.

As the police car drew near the tiny village police station, young boys and girls, playing nearby looked at the van with curiosity. The local police Inspector, Mr. Karpure was waiting for them. He was feeling very important that he could get a chance to interact with Mumbai Police. He received them warmly and handed over the meager file which he had kept ready on the table. The FIR filed said that their daughter Jamuna, 25 year old was missing for the past one month. She was supposed to have gone to Mumbai but they did not have any address of her working place. The parents had gone to Mumbai to see their daughter looked in her earlier office, where she had worked three months back. They were informed that their daughter had quit the job three months back and joined some other office. They did not have her address of her residence. There was one photograph of the girl attached to the complaint. Jadav stared at the photograph. It was Jessica. She had changed the name from Jamuna to Jessica for the glamour world.

Jadav and Inspector Kote took the local address, and walked to her house. It was a small, brick house, near their farm. Jamuna's mother was at home. Seeing the Police duo she sobbed bitterly and between her sobs she managed to say, "Jamuna was very good looking and was always interested in joining the film line wanted to be the next Deepika. She went to nearby town, and did her studies until BA. Then she went to Mumbai. She had given us this address. She never used to write any letter but called us in the neighbour's landline phone every week. She has stopped calling for past three months. But we were getting her money every month. As she was not answering the phone calls, her father and I went to the office address, given to us. Then we were in for a shock. No one knew which office she was working at all or where she was living! But then how is she sending us the money regularly?" The mother broke into uncontrollable sobs. Jadav looked at her with sympathy and said, "We will do our best to find her. Please do not worry"

As they got into the car, Kote looked at him with questioning eyes. Jadav said "Jamuna was killed three months back. Someone was still sending the money regularly to avoid any suspicion. While the criminals had collected the dead body and cremated, her real parents were here still waiting, hoping to get some information day after day. Why break their hearts just now by telling them the painful truth? So I did not tell her anything. Hope keeps people going." The car moved back to Mumbai this time slowly.

Chapter 8

The diary

Jadav was highly irritated, helpless and exhausted. He muttered in a low voice "This case is absolutely baffling, driving me crazy. Every evidence or lead is so perfectly wiped off and worse than that, we don't even know the real parents of these girls. Every where we are ending up with a dead end." Kote said "Sir, remember that anonymous letter mentioned specifically 'a tall girl'. Ritu according to the record, was five six. That means this girl we are looking for should be around five nine or ten"

Jadav said "What are you trying to say Kote? In this human ocean, how can you search for a girl just knowing her height whose face is unknown? For all this the killer girl may be planning for her next murder – heaven knows which innocent girl this time!!'

The telephone on the table started ringing. Inspector Kote picked up and said "Hello" As he listened his face relaxed into a smile and he nodded at Jadav as he answered "Thank you so much for the help. We will be there in ten minutes." Keeping the receiver back he turned to Jadav and nearly shrieked "Sir it was a call from the travel agency where Ritu worked. They had a found a diary of Ritu just today." Even before he could finish Jadav was already on his feet, darting towards the car, and Kote ran behind him.

Mr.. Bakshi was waiting for the officers. He said "Sir, today we were getting pesticide done to our office. As all the tables were moved, we found this diary tucked behind Ritu's table! May be it had fallen out from the drawer and the relations who emptied the drawers had missed it. On your last visit, you were looking for some belongings of Ritu So I thought........."

Before he could finish his long explanation Jadav snatched the diary impatiently from his hand and quickly skimmed through the pages. Then he said "Thank you so much Mr. Bakshi. You have no idea, as to what a great help you have done" They jumped back into their car. He looked at Kote and said "Pray God that the killer girl is not making her next move before we reach her" His voice sounded a bit choked. Their car stopped at the signal. Just next to them an auto came and stopped. Inside that auto was Shredha leaning on the shoulder of Meera the tall girl they were searching. Meera was calmly planning in her mind about her next job, planning.. Who should be hired to finish Shredha at the crowded Mahalaxmi station.

Back in the police station Inspector Kote and Jadav sat and started reading the diary of Ritu, in a hurry. Ritu had systematically recorded almost every day in the diary. The initial pages did not have anything important to note. From the 13th Jan it was there......

13th Jan:	*Today I had made a new friend Meera. She is so sweet. She seems to be very rich. She says her uncle is a film producer.*
15th Jan:	*Meera and me have become such thick friends. Every day she brings some chocolate for me. She frequently goes abroad and she had loads of them.*
18th Jan.:	*Meera had promised to get me a role in her uncle's serial in TV. May be next week - I will go for the audition.*
23rd Jan:	*Today Meera was my angel. God only knows how I got the stomach cramps!!. Thank God!! She took me to the doctor.*
29th Jan.	*Since I started taking the medicine I am not feeling OK. But the doctor said, I had to take them to solve my problem. I am also putting on lots of weight. I hate it.*
3rd Feb:	*Thank God now I need not take the medicine. |Meera is refusing to take the money she had paid for the medicine. But I had picked up one medical receipt, without her knowledge. I will see that I pay it back, someday..*
5th Feb:.	*How lucky- Mr. Robins of our office was trying his new camera two days back. He had clicked Meera as she came in with me. He gave me a copy. I will surprise Meera with that! She has always said she hates selfies when I ask her.*

The diary ended there. Ritu was killed in the accident of 8th of Feb. Jadav turned the diary up and down, feverishly. He shook it vigorously to see if anything is kept in between the pages. His hands were shivering and his mouth was drying. But nothing fell out. He again started looking carefully at the front and back cover. Then they found it. A prominent bulge on the backside cover caught his attention. He put his hand inside the cover and pulled it out. It was a crushed medical shop bill and a creased photograph. He stared at the photograph. She was very much there, the tall girl! She was standing close to the innocent smiling Ritu almost hugging her as if she was her best friend in the world.

At the same time a few miles, away Shredha stood puzzled. She could not understand why on earth Meera got so irritated! It was true that both of them had planned to go to Mahalaxmi in the evening to see some friend of Meera. Unexpectedly, an old colleague of her office died in the morning, and the whole office was going for the funeral. Thus Shredha could not join Meera as planned and when Meera came to the office she told this thing to her. Shredha was wondering heart in heart "Oh god, why Meera became so angry and had to leave in such a huff!! After all, we were just going to see a friend in Mahalaxmi which could be planned for any other day. Oh god, I had never seen the ever sweet soft spoken Meera getting so angry!" She joined the office group for funeral, still confused. Shredha hardly knew that her own funeral was at hand's length and by sheer luck she escaped! A fuming, angry Meera was going in an auto, cursing all the way "What an idiot of a girl. So stupid of her to refuse coming with me! Now I have to call back all my men, waiting in Mahalaxmi. It is so painful, that I had to plan everything once again for another day"

Chapter 9

The hunt starts

Jadav and Kote were dressed in casual wear. They got out of the car and started looking for the medical shop. They located the shop. It was a rather small shop and there were a few customers there. Jadav approached the counter and asked one of the assistant. "We would like to talk to the owner of this shop. Is he here?" The assistant looked up at the man sitting at the back of the shop and said "Sir, some people want to talk to you" As the man got up, and walked toward them, Jadav's police eye, quickly scanned him from top to bottom.

He was a man in mid fifties, a bit short and plump. His face was round and chubby. His hair was balding at the temples, but the remaining hair gleamed dark black, with excess oil. His eyes however had a genuine kindness about them. He walked to Jadav, and said, "Sir, I am Banerjee, the owner of this shop. What can I do for you sir?" Jadav pulled out the crumbled, medical receipt and showed it to Banerjee and said, "Does this bill belongs to your shop?"

Mr. Banerjee looked at the receipt for two seconds, looked at the date and promptly said "Yes Sir, this is my shop bill. As you can see from the date of the bill, it is an old bill issued quite some time ago. I personally wrote it, and it was issued against a proper doctor's prescription. But is there any problem Sir? Why are you people, enquiring about this bill?"

Jadav looked around. There were no other customers. They had chosen the shop wisely. He pulled out his identity card and flashed it. Banerjee's face changed expression and he said" Sorry Sir as you two are dressed in plain clothes, I could not... Sir Please, do come inside my office. We can talk there." His office was a small room at the back of the shop. Files and bills etc were neatly filed, in glass shelves. Stocks of medicines were stored in a clinical precision. Banerjee pulled a chair and Jadav sat down. Banerjee remained standing, anxiety written all over his face as he said "Tell me Sir, what is the problem?"

Jadav said "Mr.. Banerjee, have a look at this prescription. Could you kindly tell me some details about these medicines prescribed here? Could you tell me these are given for what type of ailment?" Banerjee nervously looked once again at the receipt and said "Sir, these are pills given to women who have some gynecological problems or complicated pregnancies"

Now, Jadav looked shocked. He looked at Kote who was having nearly the same reaction. Jadav cleared his throat and suppressing his surprise calmly asked again "Do you think by any chance is this pills would be prescribed for some other problems in young girls, like some serious stomachache etc?"

Banerjee shook his head strongly and said "No Sir, never. Any stomach ache or things like that would never be treated with these pills." The question hung heavy on Jadav's head, "But why should an unwed young girl was treated with these medicines for stomach ache? Why??"

Jadav snapped out of his mental chaos, and pulled out the out of focus photograph and showed it to Banerjee and said "Please look at this snap. This tall girl standing on the right side, have you seen her any time?" Though the snap was not clear and the photo crumpled, Banerjee did not have to make an effort to identify. He answered instantly "Oh This girl! She is Doctor Meera. She works for some nearby clinic. She regularly comes to buy medicines. She says women who undergo treatment for Gynecological problems are a little uncomfortable, buying these medicines in common shop. Moreover these medicines are not available with normal chemists. Dr Meera generally telephones and places the order for the medicines in advance and then collects it for her patient"

Anger fuming from the pit of his stomach Jadav said with clenched teeth "Are you sure that she is a doctor? Are you aware as to where this doctor works? What is her clinic's address? Or any other information as to where she lives?" Banerjee now started sweating profusely. "No sir, I had never asked. Sir, is something wrong? I had not done anything illegal, sir!" Jadav said, dropping his voice to a throaty whisper "This lady is a criminal. She is not a doctor at all as she claims and neither has she worked for any legal medical centre. She is engaged in serious criminal activities. For the time being, you are the only one, who has seen her. So you better cooperate with us, or you could be also arrested as a partner in crime"

Banerjee seemed be visibly shaken. His voice shivered as he managed to say "Please Sir, I am innocent. I would do anything you ask me. Sir, I believed that she was a real Doctor and gave the medicines as per the Prescription. Sir, anything you ask me for this mistake, I will do for you!"

Jadav leaned towards Kote standing near him and had a whispered conversation. Then they started explaining things to Banerjee giving him clear cut instructions. They told him what he should do when the lady either phones or appears in the shop. Banerjee was still in a state of shock, and kept blankly staring. For a long time after Jadav had left, he still sat, slumped in his chair, motionless as the time ticked off.

Meera was talking on her mobile "Ok boss. Another scapegoat will come after two days. I will get the medicines, today only. Ok then …". She closed the call and called another number, and said, "Hello Mr. Banerjee! I need one more quota of the usual medicine". She listened and spoke again, "Oh really? You have the medicine already? So surprising! I will pick it up tomorrow by ten o' clock". She ended the call. The moment her call ended, Banerjee picked up cell phone waited for two seconds, to calm himself, and then called Jadav.

Chapter 10

The trap

As soon as Jadav got the call from Banerjee, he called his team. The group was given explicit instructions about their jobs. Next day, at nine thirty, the team was ready in front of Om Medical shop. One of the police man was disguised as a street side shoe repair man. He was dressed in an old shirt and a small shop was set up in front of him with some old shoes spread in front. A second one was a paanwalla who was busy preparing his paans. Two police men in plain clothes were standing near him as customers.

Mr. Banerjee got a call from Meera, "Mr. Banerjee, please keep the medicines packed and ready. I am in a hurry and have no time to wait in the shop." Mr. Banerjee managed to keep his voice normal and earnestly said "Of course Madam, I will pack and keep it ready along with bill. It would take only one minute for you to pick it up." His face started sweating again. He gulped a glass of water and came out of his shop. He looked around. He saw the assorted set of carefully placed people standing around his shop. Mr. Jadav and Kote, dressed in plain clothes were trying their best to look a bit shabby with their hair uncombed and ruffled. They stood near an old car reading a local newspaper. Mr. Banerjee looked at the paanwalla, and raising his voice said, "Hey paanwalla, get my Meeta Paan quick" and walked back to his shop. Jadav immediately, alerted his team on his hidden mike "All be ready, the bird is coming"

After ten minutes, an auto pulled up in front of the shop. The tall Meera, got out of the auto. She was naturally tall, about five ten and added to that she was wearing about three inches heel. Hence, she did look very tall. She was dressed in inconspicuous, ordinary girl Indian clothing. She was clad in a short white kurti, and a pair of jeans. Jadav carefully watched her face. Only the side profile was visible for him. Even then he could easily make out that she is not an Indian. Her face had a definite structure of some different race but he could not decide about the origin quickly. Though she had a very fair pink skin she was not definitely an American or English. Who was she?

As Jadav's mind raced with thoughts the lady got down. She appeared very cool and calm, no anxiety, or apprehension, was seen in her face. She calmly instructed the auto, to wait for her, and checking her purse, pulled out her cell phone and started walking towards the shop. The shop had about seven steps and she walked with ease, seem to be quite comfortable in her high heels. The auto driver thought of having a paan, and he pulled his auto to a side and got out. Mr. Banerjee trying to buy time pretended to be busy, looking into some register. The tall girl walked confidently, climbed the steps of the shop one by one. Just when she was reaching the last step, her cell phone started ringing. She stopped walking, and looked at the number of the calling person. There was a bit of surprise in her face as she answered the call, "Yes boss, I am in the medical shop as per plan. Why are you calling Boss? What is the urgency??" She heard the other side for a second and then exclaimed "Oh. God!! Is that so? Yes Sir I will do it immediately." With a shocked expression, her eyes surveyed the area around the shop. Most unexpectedly, shocking the group of Jadav, she suddenly turned back and started running down the steps of the medical store. Before Jadav could react, a speeding car came screeching in, and the car door threw open near her. A hand stretched out from the car, and tried to pull the girl in, as the car kept moving, without lessening the speed. Jadav and his team, taken by surprise, rushed towards the car. Jadav opened fire in the air, as he ran towards the car shouting "You better freeze! Or I will shoot" As the girl was running in a hurry, the heel of her shoe, got caught in the carpet on the last steps, and held her back. Now she could not make it to the moving car! Once the girl failed to climb in, the hand from inside the car, which was so far, trying to pull her, suddenly, pushed her down, and the car accelerated with maddening speed. As the car door slammed shut, the girl rolled down. Just in a second the back wheels of the car crushed her and the car sped away. Within fraction of a second a sudden, curious crowd, gathered all around and prevented, Jadav from shooting, at the car tires. He came running to the bleeding girl. The portion below the neck of the girl was totally crushed.

The police group gathered around and stood silently, unable to talk anything. Kote said, "Sir, Shall we take her to the hospital and try out something?" Jadav shook his head and in replied in a dejected voice "No use Kote! Dead people will not talk." He looked again at the girl in pool of blood.

The out starched fair hand still had the topaz ring in that. Kote said in a meek voice "Sir, that car must have been parked in the corner of the road, and waiting. How did they know about our plan Sir?"

Jadav sighed deeply and said "Kote, these people must be always tailing her, to help in case of emergency. But today they should have noticed our group, became suspicious, and could have decided to tell her to quit the place. Their aim was only to pick up their agent, but unfortunately she slipped and died. She was the only single lead for us in this case, and we had lost her also." He turned around, and looking at the waiting group and said, "Telephone for the ambulance and remove the body and complete the other needed formalities" He walked back to his car.

Kote, excused himself saying "Sir, please one minute." He ran back to the auto rickshaw, who was all dazed and still standing there and thundered, "You stupid fellow, you stupid pan loving idiot, if you had not re parked your auto, and if it was standing were the lady told you to on the road. The car could not have room to enter, and this lady would not have got killed! All because of you….." As the driver trembled he walked back to the car, with a strange satisfaction, that he had taken out his anger on someone. He got into the driver's seat and looked at Jadav and said "Sir, Shall we?" And the car roared into full speed.

Chapter 11

A New Strategy

Ten days had passed after that incident. Jadav never spoke a single word about the incidence and this calm unnerved Inspector Kote. Today, Jadav called him to his room. As Kote entered, he noticed the usual rock faced, unemotional Jadav, for a change, was looking a bit cheerful today! He looked up at Kote and said "Kote, we are going to start the investigation of the girl's mysterious murders all over again, but from a new angle. Come in and sit." Kote walked in and sat. Jadav did not say anything further and he waited silently. Seconds passed. Jadav seemed to be waiting for someone. The old fashioned, wall clock (some things never change in police stations!) started striking, breaking the silence, and finished ten beats. There was a knock at the door. The door opened, and a lady police officer entered, walking with quick brisk steps. Her shoes clicked as she saluted Jadav and said "Sir, crime inspector Sherya Kale reporting Sir"

Jadav said "Come in Sherya, I am just waiting for you. Take a seat please". Kote gulped, and could not help staring, at the new officer. To begin with, even in his wildest dreams, he could not have thought, that a tough iron guy like Jadav, would involve a lady crime officer in his group. Secondly, the striking beauty of the young officer was making his heart race in a mad frenzy. She looked more of a young cine star than a police officer. Her flawless milky, fair complexion, glowed, in the dull light of the room. Her perfect chiseled face, sharp nose, and her striking blue eyes..she could give stiff competition to world beauties. Her short hair was tightly tucked, under her cap. But a few errant curls that had escaped out of the cap danced on the nape of her neck like dark satin curls.

As Kote shook his head visibly to stop staring shamelessly, Jadav was busy briefing Sherya about the case and the progress they had done so far. Kote wiped his face and leaned forward to focus on what Jadav was saying. Now Jadav turned to Kote and said "I hope I have covered all points, right Kote?"

Kote gulped and stammered, "Oh yes sir, you have described everything. "Ok then" Jadav instructed "Sherya, first you go to hospital and meet Dr. Mitra, the Surgeon, and complete the procedure. Then the lady help would get you ready for the action. After all these procedure you will meet me in said place at four o' clock sharp. He did not mention the name of the hotel but scribbled it in a note pad and showed her. Without asking a single question she got up and said "Yes Sir. I would follow your orders" She saluted again and walked out.

Jadav looked back at Kote with a contemptuous look and said "You stared at Sherya for exactly three minutes and twenty seconds. You thought that I was not noticing?" Kote's face turned deep red as he stammered, "No.. No Sir. I was trying only to ...." Jadav picked up his cap and said "She is a brilliant officer, and had worked with me in one of my previous case. I selected her because along with a great intelligence, she is also quite a beauty. We need that especially in this job. Ok, come along. We have some ground work to be done before we meet Sherya, again". He got up and adjusted his cap smartly and started walking out and Kote hurried to follow.

At four o'clock sharp Kote and Jadav reached a small roadside Dhaba on the high way. It was a very unassuming, old hotel and had hardly any customers at that time of the day. Mostly the customers who visited that Dhaba were truck drivers driving long distances, who stopped late at night for their dinner. Jadav was aware of this fact. Both the police men were dressed in casual dress. White kurties and dhotis and a colourful *'pakadhi'* as head gear. As they sat down a taxi rolled by and parked. Three young flamboyant girls looking like young starlets alighted and walked out to their table. Looking at their striking beauty, the waiter who approached the table stood open mouthed forgetting to talk. Jadav looked up at the bulging eyes of the lean server boy with a bit irritation and ordered cold drink for all. He waited two minutes for the boy to leave and then he turned to the girls and said "Yes girls now we can talk" The girl in the centre started talking

"Sir, I had finished with the assigned work with Dr. Mitra and the makeup artists had a finished their job, I think I myself cannot recognize me" She smiled. It was only then that Kote realized that this was Sherya. Jadav said "Yes, a very good job. Even I cannot recognize you." Sherya was now looking like a model straight out of the glamour magazine. She had long brown hair, which glimmered with few red streaks. Her eyes were dark brown now. She wore a bit heavy make up along with chunky large earrings, long dangling chains, and a clutter of metal bangles and beads. A tight bright T shirt along with a pair of faded jeans, added to the glamour quotient. The eager server boy came back fast with the cold drinks. They remained silent again till he placed the drinks on the table and turned back.

When he left Jadav took out a funky looking gem studded cell phone from his pocket and said "Now start using this cell phone. I have stored my unofficial number in this as BF. Be very careful at each and every step though you have to pretend, to be a little silly young girl, who can fall as an easy victim. These two officers will be with you till we pick up the target. Then you will be on your own". Jadav now took out a brown envelope and placed it on the table and said "Here are all the records needed for your new identity. You got a train pass, a Library membership card, an ATM card, some hotel bills and shop bills, all in the name of Preity Agarval, which will be your new identity. There is a receipt for six month rent payment for a single room, studio apartment, in Andheri where you will be dropped today. You will be staying in this place during the mission time. The room is equipped with everything you may need but for a computer. Keep on travelling between Dadar and Andheri frequently, and once in a while by other suburban trains. You will be working in the shop "Fashion Mall" as a counter sales girl, till we get spotted by our target. Any urgent, vital communication to me, should be through the lady selling vegetables just at the foot of your building or the old cleaning lady at the mall. Your Code word is also given in the envelope. Study them carefully."

For all this talk, Sherya was quietly listening without uttering a single word. Finally she said "Yes Sir". As she extended her left hand to pick up the envelope and cell phone, Kote saw a fresh, surgical dressing on her left hand wrist. There was a bluish red swelling, all around the area. Jadav looked at the dressing for two seconds and said "Looks like your skin had shown some allergic reaction, to the insertion. Still, try to remove the dressing as early as possible" Sherya nodded and got up. All through all these conversation, the other two girls were sitting silently. Now the three girls walked back to the taxi laughing and giggling a bit loudly drawing the attention of any one around

Jadav looked at Kote and said "Since we had lost the lead, we are now placing a bait to get the target moving towards us. Hope this time we will not miss" Both of them got up and walked to the parked old car, with paint peeling and a lot of dents on its body. It was a special car, which Jadav use for such special missions. He always thought it was lucky.

Chapter 12

The Research Center

10 months back -

It was a busy morning in the ***"Ramayya Research and Development Centre"*** of Bangalore. This was considered as one of the biggest DNA research centre in India. It was engaged in major research work of DNA isolation, and modification of Genes and their pattern. The dean of the centre, Dr. Bhaskar Raju, was busy at his work. His eyes were glued to the monitor, projecting images, of DNA, which was achieved by a specially designed, latest developed technology. The image of DNA was magnified to a million times its size, and such there was no need to have a cluster of them as in early days for the research. Bhaskar was trying to identify a specific trait from the long chain of DNA. He had been aggressively trying for the past two hours, changing the angle, rotating it, changing the plane etc but he was not able to get, what he was looking for. He pushed his chair back from the monitor, and shook his head with dejection. Utter disappointment was pasted all over his face. His already weak eyes were burning now and he decided to take a break.

He walked to one of the many large fridges, placed on the side of the vast laboratory and picked up an eye drop bottle. Sitting in his chair, he put the drops in his eyes and closed them. Though he had closed his eyes, the funny shaped DNA pattern, he was viewing, was still dancing tantalizingly in his head. He was restless. He had to insert a tiny change in the loop so that the quality of the gene would change drastically as he wanted. For past one month, he was working on this project, and till now he was not able to make any headway. The images haunted him day and night, tormenting him all along. He was close, he knew it, but it was so frustrating. He needed a strong filter coffee break.

He was about to ring the bell when the lab assistant entered. He was wearing a white colored sterilized anti bacterial suit and a mask, like everyone else. He walked softly towards Bhaskar, his rubber shoes hardly making any noise, and whispered through his mask "Sir, some high official from military intelligence is waiting in your cabin for past ten minutes. Is it possible for you to you come down Sir?" Bhaskar looked up and blinked his tired, overworked eyes and yanked out his mask. "Yes I am coming" he said.

He walked to the attached wash room, removed his sterile gloves and washed his hands methodically. He looked in the mirror and pushed back his just three thin silver unruly hairs, on the balding forehead and washed his face. As he mopped his weary countenance in a fresh towel, his mind now started racing with curiosity. He was not new to communication from top officials from many departments, once in awhile. But most of their interactions happened over the phone or through emails, or a in a meeting of group of officials together. This was the first time a high ranking officer was personally visiting him. Why should a senior officer from military intelligence, personally come in to visit him, that too so suddenly without notice? Speculating various possibilities, he walked ahead opening one by one three huge air tight doors of the sterile lab till he reached his office cabin.

As he entered the man seated in the visitors chair got up. He was a well built man, very tall, may be six feet and seven or eight inches, and looked almost like a African sportsman. He was almost towering over Bhaskar as he stood there. He had a very fair complexion and looked an unusually strong muscled man, his muscular shoulders and hands bulging under his dress, and his face had some shades of a different, unusual clan, which Bhaskar could not place immediately. Is that Turkish or Arab?? Bhasker's mind was pondering. The gentleman smiled and extended a hand and said "I am Tippu Chinnayya. I am the chief of the special project, just created in the Army intelligence sector. It is a pleasure meeting a great scientist like you" After a strong handshake, they seated themselves and then over two steaming cups of coffee started their discussion.

As Bhaskar heard more and more, about the reason of his visit to this office, his heart started racing with boundless happiness and unexplained emotion. After half an hour of meeting the officer shook hands and left. But Dr Bhaskar still sat in his chair thinking. After twenty minutes of deep thought he picked up the phone and dialed an internal number. As the voice of his admin head answered, he asked, "I am sure you checked the credentials of the Mr. Tippu before you permitted him to come and meet me?" His Admin officer answered "Yes Sir, we double checked. Actually he called on yesterday for an appointment but we kept him pending and we checked over the Internet, and also talked to the our contacts, the intelligence head. It is true that our Army has created a new research wing. This project is highly confidential. All the paper work, signature are all clean" Dr Bhaskar said "OK thank you" and kept the phone back. Holding such high posts called for lot of vigilance and he always believed in counter checking.

Most of the nights, it was difficult for Bhaskar to fall asleep. His over active brain made him restless and he was compelled to take some sleeping pills to get a few hours sleep. But to night, he had all the reasons to remain awake and ponder. Fifteen years back when Dr Bhaskar joined as a senior research fellow in the DNA department, he had many dreams. But as days progressed he found that though he had the intelligence for outstanding research he and his team were restrained by the red tape administration. There was always a lack of needed fund to have a free hand in the research. Today when Dr Tippu told him about his appointment as a head in the DNA research lab for the military, the most wonderful word he heard was "Total freedom for research and unlimited fund to do so" Then other conditions mentioned seemed trivalent and he did not even think over them seriously. Next day morning he has to pick six or eight of his best assistants, to join him in his new venture. Surprisingly, he fell asleep without any medicine.

Next day he had a meeting with his ten young s scientist doctorates who were working with him. He put forward the unusual proposal of the project. He said "Friends, we are offered a once in a life time opportunity of working for a research project. The aim of the project and the party who is sponsoring, are all highly classified, and will not be disclosed to us at any time. The research we would be doing would be on the same lines of what we are doing now. The best part of this project would be that we would have full freedom of our work, unlimited amenities, and a free, unrestricted, atmosphere to work. For the six months of our service we would be paid a huge amount in dollars as remuneration and half of which would be credited to our bank account before we leave. There is only one condition which may be a bit difficult for some of you….." He stopped his speech and looked around. The young smart doctors were smiling ear to ear. All said and done the scientists and professors never get paid so high. No wonder this news was a real stroke of luck. One by one they started "Sir, tell us the condition. We cannot wait" D.r Bhaskar cleared his throat and said "All of us would be staying, living in a special research centre day and night. We would be totally, cut off from the outside world. No one would be allowed to use a cell phone, or telephone and no one should, make any contact with their friends or families or any one, outside the centre. No one should disclose to your family or friends about the project. All our necessary things, clothing, food, medical would be taken care of by the research centre. Once the research is completed we can return to our position back to this office"

There was a dead silence for two seconds as the shocked scientists tried to digest the bitter part of the news. Then a murmur of voices started. Dr Bhaskar, had anticipated this, and he waited patiently. Then a senior doctor, Dr. Hemant, the next in line to Bhaskar, said "Dr Bhaskar, don't you think this proposal looks a bit hazy and tricky? Confidential and high level classification etc are all understandable. We have worked in many such projects. But no communication with family, friends? How can anyone think, that Scientists of our caliber can leak any information?"

Dr. Bhaskar said "Great things come with a price tag. That is why I am not forcing any of you to join unless you are comfortable in doing so. All of you think well, take your own time to decide, and let me know your answer by tomorrow" Seven of the young doctors were single and they were ready to jump at the offer. Three of them were married and settled with children. They were a bit confused, and finally thinking of the larger interest, and huge cash reward, and their family's future, they gave in. All of them told their homes that they were going for a project abroad, and might be out of touch for two to three months (As told to them wisely by Dr Bhaskar).

After fifteen days one fine morning the team of doctors, boarded a special bus with Dr Tippu, without any luggage, cell phone or camera, carrying with them, only their hope of a new world of research, and fame and happiness.

Chapter 13

The Fish

It was three days since the Preity Agarval and her friends started travelling up, and down by train. They were a noisy bunch, talking loudly about movies, chances in getting role in TV and their auditions. The women in the compartment never failed to notice the stunning Preity and even if they had not noticed her, the juicy talk of her offers to act in some TV serial and how she was waiting for the right break made heads turn and acknowledge her beauty. Today a young girl boarded from Andheri along with them. Preity pretended to be immersed in her incessant of blabbering, but her eyes were carefully watching the new girl. She was standing out from the rest of the crowd, because of her foreign features. She was well built, good height. She was dressed like a starlet, red highlights in her hair, lot of jingling jewelry in the hand and neck, and a constant chewing of gum in the mouth. She wore extra large sunshades, which she never removed. Preity could see that this girl was listening with rapt attention, to every word spoken by the three girls and hiding behind her large shades, she was actually looking at them all the time.

At the next station as some women got down, she moved to the side and purposely bumped into Preity. She flashed a big smile and said, "I am so sorry." With that, she started a conversation with Preity. Soon they all alighted in Dadar station. Preity sent a two-word message to Jadav, through the cleaner woman, which said, "Fish hooked."

Three more days and Preity found that the girl, who called herself Meera, waited for her every day and travelled with her, and became very friendly with her. She said that her uncle was looking for a new face for his next movie and Preity looked perfect for it. She promised to introduce her uncle to Preity as soon as he returns from is US trip. She gave some foreign chocolates every day to Preity. Preity pretended to revel in the divine taste of these chocolates, while she secretly pocketed the sweet in her purse.

On the fifth day of their meeting, after a few minutes of eating the chocolate ritual, Meera asked her if she was feeling ok. Preity got the message. In a few minutes, as if by cue, she suddenly doubled, complaining about strong pangs of pain. Meera helped her to visit the nearby doctor. The Doctor checked her, gave her medicine and asked her to come after one week for follow up to see the cysts in her uterus.

Jadav sat in his office with his team of his juniors planning the operation. They had the exact location of the said doctor's clinic, from the computer chip, which was placed inside Preity's wrist by the surgeon. Jadav decided to raid the doctor's nursing home when Preity is inside the clinic, so that they could collect enough evidence against the criminals. The so-called doctor's clinic was in a narrow lane, crowded with shops and hawkers on the platform. Hence, they decided to wait in the tail end of the lane, where the lane joined the broad high way.

A very sick, unwell Preity was helped out of the Auto by Meera. She held her tightly as she helped her to walk inside the clinic. Preity collapsed panting, in the first chair itself just at the entrance. Faking weakness, she closed her eyes. Meera left her there and went inside. Immediately Preity picked her phone and dialed the number. She said, "Sir we are almost there"

As she was talking, suddenly, it started pouring heavily. People on the road, ran for shelter, and many of them climbed up the long steps, of the clinic for the shelter from rain. A middle-aged woman wiping her face with her hand spotted Preity. She stared, at her for two to three seconds and then ran towards her shrieking in delight "Sherya madam? You have quit the police job Madam? You look so different now...like a movie star!" This unexpected turn shocked Preity for a second, but immediately collecting her cool she managed to look calm. She showed a deliberate, surprised expression, and giggled like a teenager "Police? You are mistaken me for someone else I think. I am a TV actress, and my name is Preity Agarval. You could have seen me in one of the serials, where I act as police women. Probably you got confused because of that."

On the other side, Jadav was still on the open line. Hearing this conversation he jumped up from his chair and muttered in desperation "Oh God. Give me a break! How did the devil of this lady identify Sherya?"

In the nursing room, the confused woman, was not very sure now. Still wiping her face she looked at Preity intensely again and stammered "I am so sorry Madam. You look so much like one Police officer who did a great help for me. I am so sorry." By this time, the rain had stopped and the lady walked down the steps, and disappeared in the crowd.

Preity got up and looked around. Luckily, no one had noticed what had happened just now. She sighed with relief, and quickly moved to a large sofa, kept in the inner side of the reception, and started talking again, "Uncle, some silly aunty thought I was police. You know ...." Before she could finish her sentence, some thing, very hard, hit her on the back of her head. In a second, she collapsed with a small muffled scream. The cell phone flew from her hand and fell in a corner.

Jadav, still listening on the other end of the phone, heard the low moan of Preity and called out desperately "Hello, Hello Preity are you all right?" There was no reply. However, the line was open and he could still hear the background noises. He heard a lot of footsteps moving around and a rough voice said "Give her an injection quickly. Make it a double dose. If she is really a police dog, then it has to be strong." More noises, chairs being dragged. Then someone stepped on the phone and crushed it deliberately with the shoes.... and then all noises ended. There was a dead silence.

Jadav was now screaming frantically, shouting orders, "Our officer is in danger! Quick! We have to move fast." He sprinted to his car, and all the others followed the suit. Even though they were waiting very close to the nursing home, just at the end of the road, jammed traffic and swarms of people walking around made it impossible to move. After six minutes when they did reach, the clinic it was closed with the rolling shutters.

Jadav looked around desperately. A small curious crowd had already gathered. He asked one man standing close by. "Did you see any one leaving the clinic?" The man answered "Yes Sir. Five minutes back a bleeding patient in a stretcher was moved in an ambulance. A nurse and a doctor also got into the ambulance. Then the clinic was shut down." Jadav ordered his men to break open the shutter, and they moved into the nursing room. One hour of painful search lead to nothing. Everything was neatly wiped off. There was not even a single fingerprint. Preity's brutally crushed phone was the only evidence left there, almost as if to taunt him.

Back at his station, Jadav opened his PC and struggled, to trace the chip inserted in Sherya's hand. For some queer reason, he was not able to get any signal from the chip. There was no sign of Sherya. He called up the technical section, which provided the electronic chip. The tech department was also surprised, that the chip had stopped tracking. The expert said "Sir, it is very, very unusual sir that the chip fails to send a signal. The only possibility is, I am very sorry to tell you this that your officer might have been injured very badly, and the chip got …disconnected from the body. I am very, very sorry sir"

Jadav sat back with a heavy heart. Somewhere deep inside his heart, he felt a deep hurt. "Poor girl. So young! Foolishly, I unnecessary risked her life" he cursed himself. He sank deeply into his chair and stayed on in the station without going home. He was awake until two thirty in the night, with the guilty conscious killing him. Latter still sitting his chair, he fell into a disturbed sleep. A sharp, beep, beep noise, made him jump up. He rubbed his eyes and tried to find the source of the beep. As he saw the green dot moving on the screen of his, still open laptop. He jumped up, and looked at the screen. The signal was now moving slowly. He looked up and said "Thank you God, Thanks for saving Sherya" He punched some keys of laptop and could get India map on the back of the signal. He zoomed and focused at the point of the blinking green dot. Reading, the latitude and longitude, Jadav could make out that she was moving, somewhere near Karnataka.

Chapter 14

A boon for the village

Eight months back—

It was a small village at the interior part of Karnataka. It was the usual morning routine of the village: milking the cows, collecting cow dung, plucking vegetables and people walking around for odd jobs. Chinna was in the cowshed mixing the cow dung in a bucket, when her neighbor, Sumi came panting in to her house. She said in an urgent voice "Chinna, leave all your jobs, wash your hands and come with me just now. Fortune is going to smile at us." She hustled Chinna and almost dragged her with great urgency until they reached the Panchayat ground. Chinna found there was a crowd already; about twenty-five to thirty women, of their village had come, and were sitting there, huddled and waiting eagerly

Chinna and Sumi sat down. Sumi still panting turned to Chinna and whispered, "Some big people from *Sarkar,* are going to offer us job with good salary. That is why we are here," A surprised Chinna asked in a surprised voice "Job? For us? What kind of job? We are village people with not much education and …" Before Sumi could answer, a small group of extremely well dressed people entered. The eager village women watched the visitors with open mouth. There were two beautiful women in western suits, pastel coats and fitted skirts, looking like they had walked out of an English movie. The Panchayat members followed them. The Panchayat president asked all of them to sit quite and listen carefully to what the ladies were to say. Then one of the women came in the front and started speaking in local language. Though the accent was difficult, she managed to talk very slowly, repeating some line again, so that they could follow. She said, "Many of you villagers are repeatedly facing crop failure, due to natural calamities, like failure of rain or un seasonal rain or other factors. The Prime Minister believes in empowering women, especially the village women. We are social workers from America. We along with your Government have decided to provide you women with employment opportunity. We are going to select some of you women who have completed some education and train you with the basic skills of nursing. You will be taught to handle emergency, dressing of a wounded person etc. On completion of training, you all will be provided with job in the same village or nearby village. Are you all happy about that?"

All the women clapped in happiness. Then the Americans made a group of women who had studied at least up to eight standards. Only fifteen of them fell into that category. The other women looked crest fallen. Then the Americans again talked among them selves and said "Ok we had selected the first level of nurses. We would also select a second level of women for the grade II nurses." Now a group of twelve was selected.

Now the Panchayat President said "This is a golden opportunity, our *Sarkar* is giving us. I want all of you to use it faithfully. Tomorrow onwards the classes will be conducted in our primary school, from eight 'o' cock in the morning to four 'o' clock in the evening. Everyone should be punctual and learn sincerely"

Back at the Panchayat office the two ladies offered the contract of the project to the Village Panchayat head. The President and his members read the clauses and conditions, written on a Government Stamp Paper, in the local language. It was stamped and signed by the Minister for Rural development. The social workers handed over a cheque for a heavy amount to the Panchayat for agreeing to the implement the project.

Next day, two vans full of basic medical equipments, teaching equipments, projection screens, projectors and three lady doctors arrived. The village women were as happy as schoolchildren coming to school. They were also happy that they fell into the age group of below sixteen which was the basic prerequisite asked by the team heads. Days rolled by and nurses level first and second learnt quickly and efficiently. The audiovisual explanation and demonstrations made it easier for them. Surprisingly they were not asked to write much, which was a great relief for the villagers. Each women was photographed, medically examined, finger prints taken and were provided with an identity card. They were also provided with four sets of nurse's uniforms, which the villagers were very proud of wearing. One month rolled by.

On that day, as the sun was rising, there was an emergency urgent call for the new nurses to assemble early in the morning at the school. The Americans told the new nurses that a major train accident had occurred between the Banglore station and their village. Hence, all of them were needed urgently to procced to the accident spot to work as volunteers. They were told to pack heir uniforms and assemble again by half an hour.

After forty minutes, the 27 nurses, the two American ladies and the doctors boarded a luxury air conditioned bus. As the family watched and bid good by, the bus roared and disappeared in a cloud of dust from the mud road. The poor villagers, not exposed to outer world, were counting happily the two thousand rupees given to every nurse as advance salary.

Chapter 15

The journey

The Ambulance moved on, non-stop. It was two 'o clock in the morning, eight hours since Shreya was hit on the head and sedated. She slowly came back to consciousness. She remained, and with shuteyes tried to recall what happened. That random woman in the crowd, identifying her as a police person, was unfortunate. She had taken so much effort to look very different and yet that woman had recognized her and blurted her identity out! Then immediately she had moved to a inner sofa to avoid another incident and just started talking to Jadav. She now recollected hearing soft footsteps behind her and before she could react, she was hit. That means, some one from the clinic was watching her all along without her knowledge, and understood, that she was a plant. It is possible that they did not kill her immediately because they did not want to take a chance when police was already tailing them. Definitely sooner or latter, they would get rid of her but before that she should act.

As per Dr Mitra's advice, she had taken an antidote injection before going to the nursing home. Hence she had woken up reasonably fast in spite of the double dose they had given her. She opened her eyes, just barely. The inside of the ambulance was quite dark. Passing road lights flickered, a mild illumination of and on. She opened her eyes fully now and looked. In the passing flickering light she could make out the outline of a nurse in uniform sitting on the seat near window, possibly to guard her. But she was in deep sleep, and swayed with the motion of the van. Shreya tried to feel around, with her hands. Being left handed, she first tried to lift her left hand. She winced with a sharp pain, as she tried to pull her hand. Now she put her right hand on the same spot, tried to grope around, and tried to feel. She wanted to figure out what was that heavy load that was sitting on her left hand wrist, hurting her. With the corner of her eyes, she could see even in the darkness that it was a carton loaded with medicines. They had put the entire carton over her left hand. Like a snake, she wriggled her hand, very, very slowly, millimeter by millimeter. Biting her lips, to bear the pain and not to make a sound, very, very, gently and finally, she pulled her hand out from the bottom of the heavy carton. She cursed the person who had placed that heavy box on her hand. What she did not know, was that all that strong chemicals in those medicine pile giving out mild radiation, had blocked so far, the signal from her wrist and had made Jadav's life miserable!

Breathing heavily, she looked at the sleeping nurse, and her dynamic brain worked with lightening speed. She rolled very slowly on her side and waited for any movement from the nurse. Finding none, she rolled again, and reached under the nurse's seat. She held her breath and listened, and waited for any movement. There was absolutely no movement from the nurse. She looked very still. Shreya's watch was intact in her hand. She pressed a side button and the watch gave out a pencil ray of light. She quickly moved her fingers through the injection vials, reading the names of medicines. She thanked God, for her training she received, as a crime officer, where they were introduced to important medicines and some nursing. She found the vial she was looking for, which was the same injection they gave her. It was kept ready on the top so that the nurse could give her another shot of the injection before she would wake up. Picking up the injection, Shreya slowly got up. Reaching the nurse from the backside, she tried to jab the needle in to the shoulder of the nurse, at the same time covering her mouth.

However, suddenly the nurse turned and slapped her very hard across the face. The sudden unexpected attack took a fraction of second for Shreya to steady herself. Instantly, the stocky nurse had pushed her down and jumped over her. The nurse was quite heavy built and Sherya was very weak, because of the drug she was injected with. She managed to hold the injection on her hand still, and tried to push the nurse. Both of them rolled over the floor repeatedly, each trying to overpower other. Sherya gathered her full strength and buckling her knees kicked the nurse in her hip. The kick was quite strong. However, the nurse still did not let her grip from Sherya's dress. Both rolled again kicked and hit each other in the narrow space, and the crowding boxes were making her movements difficult. She was becoming weaker and weaker and losing to the bulky nurse. The nurse scratched her face and punched her in the nose. For a moment, Shreya blacked out. As she opened her eyes, she found that the nurse was sitting on her and holding both her hands captured between her legs and her raised hand was coming down with the injection. Shreya tried her best to push the hand away and bend it. The nurse had a cruel glee in her face. Then there was an ear-piercing shriek as Shreya screamed in the top of her voice. The attack was sudden. Then there was total silence in the ambulance.

Chapter 16

The Strange Exhibition

Dr. Aruna was a doctorate in child welfare and rural development and was the co- director of an NGO. After a long break, post her delivery, today she was joining back for her duty. Actually, she had planned to take only two months break after her delivery. Unfortunately, her baby girl was born with some heart problems. They had to wait for three months to operate on the baby. She had stayed back, nurturing and praying fervently, taking care of the baby post the surgery. Her maternity leave had stretched to five months. Luckily, the painful ordeal was all over and her five-month bubbly daughter, Ahana was a healthy little bundle of joy.

Aruna was back in her research centre. Her secretary, Madu brought her a set of files, and smiling broadly said "Welcome back Madam. So, now you would be so happy Madam that you can go back and see your grown up babies once again! You must be thrilled." Aruna flashed her usual smile and taking the files replied, "Of course Madu, in fact I had been worried about these children of mine for past one month"

Dr. Aruna's NGO called the *"Centre for Empowering Rural Women"* was funded by the Ministry of Women and child development. Added to that, it was also generously funded by the World Health Organization. Under this project they had adopted five villages around Mysore. Aruna and her team visited these villages regularly every month. Besides taking care of their health and income, they were enabling theses village women to engage in some form of village crafts by supplying them with the needed raw materials. The centre purchased the finished products and thus the villager received some regular income. Aruna was so dedicated to her profession that everyone in the centre used to call the villagers as her children.

Dr. Aruna's car reached the village activity room. She was a bit surprised that the usual crowd of about forty beaming village girls was not there to day.

In fact, there were hardly about ten women. She went inside the shed called as the craft room and her assistants followed her with the bundle of craft raw materials. They all sat on their usual chairs. Aruna looked around and spotted the head of the village girls group, Koki. She looked up at her and asked "Koki, are the girls of the village are not informed about my coming to day? If needed, I can wait for some time. Send somebody and call the girls" Koki looked at Aruna with a surprised look and said "Madam you are not aware that eighteen girls from our village have gone to Dubai? From the neighbouring villages also girls were selected. Madam they were supposed to have come only from your office! Surprising! You are not aware of this?"

Aruna was completely taken aback. Though she was on leave, she was constantly in touch with her centre about some administrative decisions, and research work etc. How was it possible that such a major event, her girls being send to Dubai was not informed to her? Deciding to find the correct information, she told her assistants to go ahead with the routine work and walked to the Panchayat office nearby. On seeing her Panchayat President got up and beaming broadly said "Welcome madam. It is such a pleasure seeing you after a long time. You are the real God for our village! So kind of you think of picking up our poor villagers for the Dubai craft festival"

Dr Aruna now understood that some major development had taken place and she was not aware of it. May be it was controlled directly by the State, and their centre was not involved. So without showing her ignorance she sat on the chair offered and said "Because I had major crisis in my home front my centre had not informed me about this. Can you kindly tell me what it is?"

Panchayat President said in an amazed voice "You are not aware of the project madam? Really? OK. I will tell you everything in detail" He shifted himself to a comfortable position in his chair and started: "Madam it was on the 3rd of July of last year. Our villagers were waiting as usual for you ..."

Aruna mentally calculated, 3rd July was just one week after delivery when the doctors dropped the bomb shell on her saying that her baby girl was having acute congenial heart problems and would require a major surgery" From that day till the surgery was performed it was an endless visit to doctors, consultations more opinions etc, till the surgery was done successfully. Therefore, it is never possible that someone from the centre would have contacted her.

The Panchayat head noticed that she was thinking something and said "Madam, or you listening" Aruna said "Yes Sir, you please go ahead" He started again, "That day morning three cars came to our village instead of your car. A group of official looking like some officer of authority, came out and straight away came to the Panchayat. They said that there is a global village craft exhibition, which is going to be organized and the Our Government had picked up our village for the participation, because of your strong recommendation. At first we thought that they are going to collect our finished materials. But then they explained that the participants would be working their crafts in front of the visiting public in Dubai. Our village people had hardly gone out of the village. So going all the way to Dubai did not appeal to us. The visitors told us to think about the idea and left. We discussed with the village women and some of the young girls who were educated, supported the idea and said that the villager can earn a lot of money, besides a trip abroad. More and more villagers started supporting the idea. The same people came after two days and this time there were two ladies foreigners in the group. These ladies sat among the village people and explained their project. Ultimately 20 women of the villagers, became ready for the project. The visitors said because it is foreign visit, medical examination is a must for Visa. After medical examination 8 women were rejected. Actually the team they selected were all young unmarried girls, from the age of fifteen to nineteen. They were all given a sum of Rs 3000 each for buying dresses and bags for their travel. They were all photographed and finger prints were taken and their pass port and visa were made. This all took around fifteen days. Then, on 20th July those visitors took all these women in a bus to Mysore from where they would be boarding the flight to Dubai."

Aruna having never heard of any such project so for where village women are selected for a foreign travel, was getting seriously worried. Keeping her calm, she said "The exhibitions usually run for ten days to one month. But now four months are over. Did any of the women, contact their family after reaching Dubai?" The President's face showed an expression of exasperation. He said "Madam you know when people go abroad they hardly make any phone call, because it is so expensive. My own nephew is in Dubai and he only writes letters, that also once in three months. So these organizers, how can we expect them to pay all villagers for telephone calls?"

Aruna could sense the irritation in his voice and said "You are right. How can anyone make a telephone call? OK. When they first came with the proposal did they show you some documental proof about the proposal?"

Without answering her he turned and looking inside his house, called his daughter "Champa, Get that Dubai project file" As Aruna waited he added "Tell your mother to make some tea for our Madam" A young, bubbly teenage girl Champa came with a folder and handed it to her. She skimmed through the papers. The last paper was a copy of the list of girls selected for the project. The next one was a letter from Ministry of rural development, explaining about the exhibition in short. It was signed by some deputy-secretary. The letter was in English. She looked up at the President, watching her face attentively and forcing a smile and said, "Sir, this seems to be a very good project. Could I get a copy of this letter please?" The President showed all his teeth, having won the war expression, and chuckling loudly said "Of Course Madam, Of course by all means"

Dr Aruna took her cell phone and took all the pictures of all the documents. As she was getting up he added, "Madam. Oh! I forgot to mention one thing! One month after they left, a lady telephoned me and informed me, that all the village women are safe and the exhibition will go on for about three to four months. One more thing you know Madam, All those ladies who came were Americans and were wearing suits in the village! Were looking so out of place" He chuckled on for reasons known only him. Refusing the invite for tea, Aruna excused herself and walked back to her craft room.

Next day she called her secretary and asked her to verify about the project. She transferred her cell phone image to her laptop, and asked her secretary to send it as attachments for verification to the secretary of rural development ministry. After two hours of contacting various offices her PA came back and said that no such letter was issued from the Ministry and there was no such deputy who had signed the letter.

Dr. Aruna took an appointment from Commissioner of Mysore. She travelled to Mysore next day and met the Commissioner of police and discussed everything with him. He carefully studied the printout of the documents brought by her. He called his PA and gave him some quick instructions. As the PA left the room he turned to Dr Aruna and said "Madam, this one seems to be a big ring of crime operation! It might be possible that people who came pretending to be US persons, and recruited women, in fact might not be Americans at all. The may be belonging to human traffic gang and using the ignorance of the villagers, had lifted these women. Since you say that some women were taken from nearby villages, this issue turns out to be very serious and sensitive issue and we have to handle it very, very cautiously. If this information ever happens to leak out to the press, there would be a big uproar. Let us investigate this matter confidentially. I will get in touch with some high level officers in crime branch and start an investigation. Mean while we would issue circulars to all Panchayats that hereafter any so called project arrangement could not be done at Panchayat level, but should be referred the commissioner of police of the nearest district, and the approval can be sanctioned only after a through verification of the facts by the police department. He stopped as there was a knock at the door and his PA entered. His PA informed, "Sir, I checked all the records as per your instructions. The airport authorities had checked their records and reported that no such group of ladies had left by Dubai flight in the said three days. They had in fact, checked all the passengers of one week and of all the flights going to Dubai. No group of women every boarded on any such flight at all." Dr Aruna and the Commissioner sat staring at each other in dismay.

After two days the commissioner telephoned Dr Aruna and informed that he had enquired with Dubai Government, and as expected there was no such cottage industries exhibition held there. She reported back the commissioner that she had enquired from the UNISCO and WHO and she was similarly informed --- that no such project was carried out by any one of them in India. As the commissioner closed the line, his head started throbbing under the grave information. It was his unfortunate responsibility to handle such a sensitive, crucial, investigation. He called his PA, and told him to get an appointment for him with the head of the Crime branch section in Delhi as early as possible.

Chapter 17

The discussion

A small group of officers from crime branch sat in the conference room, brainstorming the various strategies they might have to plan for this case. On the wall, hung a large projection of India map with Karanataka region illuminated bright. There was a marker line of a green florescent pen line tracing from Mumbai to the base of some mountain range in Karnataka. The line vanished in the mountain range. ACP Jadav had already briefed the group about the development so far. He continued now "Looking at the signals from the chip placed in the hand of our officer, it is now definite that she is taken to a place somewhere near this mountain range. However, the point is that why the tracer is unable to trace her movement anymore. The chip was transmitting signal from a special secure centre from our Indian satellite. According our experts from the software, the tracer signal cannot be affected by the hill or the height of the mountain range. In addition, it is proved because the tracer had shown signal up to a good height, in the mountain. This meeting is then to decide our plan for an attack on this region because definitely this must be the den of the criminals"

The Commissioner Mr. Gadre, positioned at the head of the table pondered on this suggestion, and said "Jadav, in this case till now we are not able to zero down on the type of crime, this gang is working on. They have murdered four young girls, but there was no organ theft. The background of these girls had given us no clue at all about the crime neither it had shown any link between all the four girls. They were young girls living alone in Mumbai. That is all! Only one common factor found so far is that, they were all aspiring, to enter the glamour world. That is why our young lady officer was used as bait. We were almost close enough to catch the gang but we failed miserably! This gang now probably has our officer. Mr.. Jadav, I am sorry to say that you, one of the most smart officer, and proved yourself many times in the past but you failed here. I strongly feel that if you had been a little more quick enough in this case and had followed our officer as she just entered the nursing home, you could have got them all arrested in Mumbai just then and there! It could have been much better, is it not?'

Now every one's eyes turned towards Jadav. He was supposed to be the best, in the entire group of Mumbai crime branch. Nevertheless, he had missed now. Heart in heart, they wondered, that how he could explain this serious lapse, on his side. Jadav stood up, and glanced all around once and answered. "Sir, the group which was operating in Mumbai is just a tip of an iceberg. For that matter, I am sure that they might be just persons selected and employed at random, hardly knowing anything about the deep core operation of the gang. Murdering four young girls in cold blood, leaving behind absolutely no trail and then paying the girl's parents regularly, every month to avoid suspicion, are not very simple operation, where millions of people live. It shows a very strong network of well-knitted group with a lot of money and backup power. Our plan was that our officer Sherya should visit the clinic a few times, befriend someone, working there, and dig out information. Sherya had personally asked us not to follow her until she signals us. We had taken so much effort for her disguise. It is unfortunate that her cover blew up so easily. The moment we knew that she was attacked, we moved immediately. But unfortunately the clinic is situated in such a narrow alley, and so crowded, that we became too late"

One smart officer Mallic Shaha, raised his hand for permission and got up to speak. He started "Sir, I feel that there is a serious point here, which we are not able to address in this situation. Sir,. Once they know, that she was a police person, why they did not eliminate her immediately, which is the general practice of these criminals? Even assuming, that they did not want to knock her off, a police person, immediately, they could have done it latter! Say, after moving away a short distance from Mumbai! But they have not done so. It is proved by the signal of the chip! The big questions arises is why so?" As he sat down everyone started a whispered conversation on the question raised.

Murali Iyyer, an officer with sharp eyes and intelligence, said, "Sir, I had an opportunity to work with officer Sherya, for a short time. From that experience, I can assure you all, that she is not the one of the type who could be knocked off so easily. If the signal was continuously on till a few hours back, it only shows that she is still travelling with the criminals. Obviously they won't be carrying an injured person all along with them. It means she had either disguised herself, or had hid herself, and had travelled with them, without their knowledge,"

Kote was more relieved to hear this, than anyone was. He could not imagine, the most beautiful officer being killed so easily. Jadav said "Sir, what Murali says seems to be more possible. It is possible that Sherya purposely had travelled along with those people without trying to escape. She had possibly decided to reach the core of the operation site, to arrive at the key people involved. Hence we have to chart out a plan to attack their den right there in the mountain, which I feel would definitely involve a major operation."

The commissioner said "Karnataka is famous for various trekking mountains. At any given time there is constantly a stream of people climbing on various mountains. The criminals cannot think of having a base in such a place where so many people frequently visit. So where did our officer go?"

Jadav said "Sir, to begin with, let us start with an aerial survey of these mountain tops Sir. Any base camp cannot escape our survey team. Once we could spot their exact location we would plan our next move"

The commissioner said "I suggest that these two officers, Murali and Rohit, travel along the same path traced by the chip. Let them travel by the same road and make enquires all along the way. The criminals had used an Ambulance to avoid suspicion of the prowling eyes of the police, but people always give a second look when they see an ambulance. If the criminals have travelled up the mountain range, they should have halted at some points in these two days to get a break for food or tea. So just, keep your eyes and ears open, and collect every possible clue available. Then based on that information, we would proceed for an aerial survey." He then looked around and said "Remember all of you selected officers who here now, are a member of this operation team. Every one of you should try and get as much information, as possible about these mountain ranges." The meeting ended for the day but every member there had many unanswered questions racing in their minds.

Chapter 18

The Trek

The mountain range echoed with the noise of laughter and chitchatting as a group of about thirty college teenagers moved along the trekking path, on the side of the tall hills. These were the tallest hills in the Western Ghats. The students, both boys and girls were the ones who were ardent trekkers. They had come from various colleges situated in different parts India, just for trekking. There were two senior guides from the base camp, leading the trekking along with the group. All of these students had joined in by online registration for this camp. The trip was very professionally planned, down to the minutest detail. Two days earlier when they reached the base camp, first they were required to camp for two days. During this time, they were given guidance, special instruction, maps and their route. They were told about the safety measures they had to take, in case they were separated from the group, lost their way or got injured.

The senior guide Bangaru, was giving a lecture in a rather serious voice "Boys and girls, I am working as a guide for past twenty years and have trekked all the mountain ranges in India. Even then, I try not to trek all alone at time, venture in to completely unknown territory without adequate research or back up help. These mountains may look peaceful and fun. But they can be really treacherous. One wrong step and you are finished. In this steep mountain, if you slip just one step, you will roll down, all the way. I cannot be sure we can reach you in time if you wander too far away. I don't want to have your bones collected. Therefore, it is very important, that all of us always stick together. Walk in groups of three, or four and always keep a count of your partners. Your cell phones may not work after some altitude and hence all of you are given a distress whistle for use in need of an emergency"

With their bulging baggage, the boys and girls started climbing yesterday morning. Today was Day 2. They had rested in another base camp set up for the previous night's stay. The morning was very cool. With the lush green trees and bushes, the sight was a real treat to the eyes. It had just rained two days back and the single narrow path they trekked along was still a bit slippery. Among this group, there were three boys, who all came from Bangalore. They had purposely kept trailing at the tail end all along. They ambled along more and more slowly till they got quite separated from the group. It was their plan.

Aryan, the head of this team, had a plan of his own. Even before leaving Banglore, they had made this adventurous plan. Aryan told his friends, Dhrishya and Mohan "We will do real exploration, in the mountain. I read from the internet, that there are some deep caves on the side if the hill range. But, we won't be allowed to trek alone in this mountain valley. So we will start with the group from the base camp. Then once we start trekking, let's get separated from the group, and then we can trek freely on our own. We have to spot these mystery caves and trek through them. I read there are number of water springs, inside this cave and trekking through them, would be just awesome." Dhrisyan said "But suppose we lose our way?" Mohan laughed and said" You Mommy's baby, you don't come with us. You please sit at home" Aryan gave Mohan a tight slap, on the back and said "You don't worry. This cave is just one single long cave running parallel to our planned trekking path of the camp. Therefore, we can go through the cave and reach the top of the mountain before the group arrives, and surprise them! In case we are not able to reach the top, we can always trace back our path and comeback to the base camp." They discussed in length referred to a lot of Google map, took printouts. They took torch lights, picked up florescent caps, florescent backpacks, a long bundles of florescent rope. So even in the dark caves, they could be able to spot each other constantly and easily.

The moment the trio was sure, that they were out of sight of the group, they started running in a a perpendicular direction to the group. After five minutes of tough running through the mountain range, they started walking on the same line still horizontal. Bushes, virgin green land thickly covered this area and looked untouched so far by any human footsteps. Walking became more and more difficult. They were not able to get any grip, on the steep sloping rock. Added to this thick creepers got entangled in their step, every time. They kept struggling, and removing the creepers off their shoes, or cutting out them. But these were the modern dare devil kids, and had earlier done many trekking expeditions. So the more difficult it got, the more thrill shone in their eyes. Suddenly from nowhere, amongst the bushes, they saw the mouth, of the narrow cave. They shrieked and yelled at the top of their voice, whistled and danced, with joy at their own triumph. Then they examined the mouth of the cave.

Mohan said, "Aryan this cave is too small. We have to crawl. It won't be much fun." Aryan touched and felt the rocks on the side of the mouth of the cave, all around, carefully, and said with confidence "No Mohan, this cave is real big enough for walking. I had read it. May be some rocks, could have rolled down, and made the entrance just small. Let us get in, and move some distance. If we don't see a bigger cave, we can come back." They all agreed. They took the end of the long florescent rope, and tied it strongly to the trunk of huge tree. Then one by one, they crawled into the cave mouth holding the rope in a tight grip. They were actually crawling on all their four. It was not easy. The crawling was painfully slow. Still with the torch struck on their cap, they moved forward, inch by inch. After about twenty minutes, they could see a dim light, coming from somewhere. There excitement flared up.

Aryan said, "See there is light!. May be the cave is broadening, after some distance" Dead tired, they moved some more distance. Now suddenly the cave opened up into a large cave. They all stood up, and looked around. The cave was quite high, as high as a van could go. But what surprised them was the light they were seeing, was not a natural light, but it was from some, distant electric light. They had hardly walked two steps, when they found, a thick barbed wire fence and a gate. There was a board, which read,

"ARMY RIFLE RANGE, NO TRESSPASSING ALLOWED"

Dishyan said, "Aryan this cave is probably taken over by the military now! So we have to go back" The daring Aryan was not ready. He said, "Army puts up this board miles away, from their actual firing range, to protect people. The actual shooting range must be very far away, on the top of the hill." He examined the gate. Then beaming he said, "See this gate is not even locked properly. Let us go in" He took his pocketknife, and picking up the lock started, turning its lever.

A sudden shrill alarm, started ringing, and the boys froze. After one second they said "Come let us run" Suddenly many flash lights flashed on their faces totally blinding them and a rough voice said "Don't you know this is Army area? Who are you boys? And what are you doing here?" The boys blinked, in the light and said" Sir please put off the light" The lights were now turned to the side of the cave. The boys could see three uniformed heavy men clad in Indian military uniform standing there. On seeing the army men Aryan picked up courage and explained why they were there. The officer said "OK you boys now go back and never try to come this way again This is strictly military area" The boys turned and started crawling back. Dishyan said "What are the Army men doing in this cave?" Mohan muttered back "Who cares? We should just thank God that we were allowed to go back"

They silently crawled back. Just as the first one was about to touch the mouth of the cave, a sudden stream of water came rushing from back side and drenched them. Before they could realize what was happening, a high power electric shock hit them and the trio's bodies became still. A powerful tug from inside pulled off the florescent rope inside. After five minutes, a large volume of rocks and soil came rolling down the slope and sealed the mouth of the cave permanently.

Next day Mysore police was searching the steep rocks all day for the three missing boys, all along the usual tracks. Aerial searches with Helicopters went back and forth. But they could get no trace of the boys. After two days search, they gave up. Two large trees and thick bushes now covered the closed mouth of the cave making it invisible.

Chapter 19

The new nurse

The nurse now sat still panting heavily, with the exertion "Oh this girl" she said to herself. "She did put up a stiff resistance. Luckily, I could knock her down. She looked at her uniform. Actually, it hung very loose on her. She now searched through the medicines again and picked up another injection. This was to make sure that the girl on the floor would remain, in a confused state of mind for three days, even if she happened to get up in between, before the men had finished their job. She whispered, "I am sorry dear girl." and injected the girl again. Still a little breathless, she fell into a deep thought planning her future actions. She was a nurse on her first journey and was not very familiar with the people who were accompanying her. During the fight, the girl had scratched her face violently and her face burnt. She looked around and found a hand towel. She made it wet with the water bottle kept on the seat, and wiped her face, to soothe it. Suddenly she felt too thirsty and she emptied the entire bottle down her throat.

After one-hour journey, the ambulance stopped and there was a knock at the door. Opening the door, she kept the towel in her hand pretending to wipe her face thus covering half her face. She did not want the men to see her bruises and ask her questions. But the man who knocked the door hardly bothered to look at her direction. He said in grumpy voice, "We are getting some tea and food. Do you want to have some?" Making an effort she talked in a husky whisper and said "Yes, I would love eat whatever you get. Watching this woman without even blinking was so strenuous!" She watched the rough face of the man. He hardly made any comment and was just about to go when she asked in a hurry "Please can you tell me if there is any wash room near by. I want to use" He went out, checked and came back and said "Yes there is a wash room on the side of hotel. You can come down" He extended a hand and helped her to get down. He pointed in the direction of the dingy rest room at the back.

She walked slowly, her face still covered with the wiping cloth till reached the hotel. She almost had to limp to the washroom. Tired and drained of all strength, she splashed water on her face. There was no mirror so she still could not see how her bruises looked. She still had no clue about the destination of the hospital where she was headed. She looked all around trying to understand the topography, some clue to place where they were. All the signboards in the shops and hotel were written in some southern language. She could not be sure whether it was Telugu or Kannada. She walked back to van.

A hot dosa and masala tea really uplifted her mood and she gobbled it quickly. As the server came back to take the plate, she gave him her most enchanting smile and asked "What is this place called?" The poor boy blinked, unable to understand the language. Then she pointed her finger to the ground, and asked "Karnataka?" Unexpectedly the driver's help came back, and barked at the boy "What are you doing here? Take the plate and run off." The boy ran away and the nurse went back to her seat, still completely lost.

Chapter 20

Mid way in the jungle

Sitting on Nurse's seat very alert, fearing another attack from the girl, her body was craving for at least a short nap. Extreme fatigue and throbbing pain, all over the body were making her eyes shut. However, in her position and in this situation, she could not risk that. She took the ice-cold water bottle given at the hotel and splashed her face generously. The freezing water and the very cold air blowing from the window made her shiver a little, but she was now more alert.

Wondering about the sudden chill wind, she moved the curtain from the window, and peeped out. She saw that their ambulance was now going through a dense forest. It was pitch dark outside and there was no proper road. But the driver was steering his vehicle with ease and at good speed, showing that the driver had travelled through the path frequently. Her mind raced raising many questions "Why are they going through this jungle? Even if they are thinking of disposing the intruder girl, why travel deep into the jungle? No! They were definitely headed for some final destination. The huge crates of medicines boxes and many parcels, of sealed boxes are being taken somewhere.. for some hospital. But where? Why should anyone carry medicine for such a long distance when medicines are available in all cities?" These endless questions were swirling in her head and making headache more pronounced, but one way, it was a good exercise to her brain, and she became more and more alert.

The ambulance stopped again. About two hours since they had stopped in the hotel for tea, she approximated. There was a rapid, loud knock at the door and she got up and opened the door. She decided that it would be wise not to ask any question. They asked her to get down and she obeyed politely. The driver and his help got into the ambulance and reached the woman on the floor. They gave her one more injection and then together they lifted her from the ambulance. They got down and carrying the limp body of the girl moved a little distance into the interior of the bushes and threw her into the bushes.

She had followed them two steps behind and watched their moves. She found that they were now inside a dense jungle, covered with trees and overgrown bushes. The driver's assistant turned to her and said, "If this police dog is not eaten by the wild animals, then she would surely die searching for her way out of the jungle! Serves her well for snooping on us! Sister you can take some rest now without worrying about your patient. Go and get into the van" He gave a cracking laughter but the driver silently walked back to his driving seat as if nothing happened. She got in to the van and closed the door. A shiver ran down her spine. She knew that when work involved hardened criminals, this kind of cruel, remorseless acts were almost enjoyed. It was evident who she was dealing with. As she sat motionless almost feeling like praying for the girl now, with a big jerk, the ambulance started moving again. Sleep overpowered her finally, and she fell into a disturbed sleep. The ambulance moved on, in to the deep.

Chapter 21

Search for clues

Crime section inspectors Murali and Rohit got ready for their journey. They disguised carefully in T-shirts, faded jeans, and hiking shoes with neon laces. They tousled their short crew cut hair and tried to make some style statement like that of spike. They adorned themselves with some fancy beaded wristbands and some chunky metal chains in their neck. They took a very normal looking car, not very new, not very old, and started their journey.

They first went to the nursing home from where Sherya had been abducted. Police had sealed it. They went to a tiny tea stall facing the nursing home and ordered for tea. As the boy was making tea, Murali started a conversation with the boy. He said, "Hey cool jeans! From where did you buy it?" The boy beamed and said, "No Sir, this is not new. My owner's son is in college. He gave me this" Murali pointed to the nursing home and asked "Why is it sealed by police? Any murder happened?" The boy said "No, No Sir. Suddenly one day, many police people came. Just before they arrived, we saw that a parked ambulance starting and moving away very fast. Earlier also, so many occasions, we had seen an ambulance coming and taking away some packages and huge parcels. We never thought anything unusual at all. But after that day raid the nursing home is closed." Murali asked "Have you anytime served tea inside that nursing home? Do you know anyone who worked there?" The boy shook his head vigorously. "Sir, The doctor and the nurse all used to come by car and some people who visited them also came by very expensive cars. Some time a tall girl used to bring in some patients in auto. We have seen that the same fair girl came three - four times with patients. May be she is a nurse or a doctor. But, none of them ever ordered any tea". So again, a dead end. They paid for their tea and moved on.

They travelled through the same path. They stopped, in every teashop, newspaper stalls and public telephone booths. They could get no clue. No one had paid any attention to an ambulance going that way. The ambulance had not stopped for tea or any telephone call. They thought that may be criminals went to some discreet place their usual halts away from normal places! They had already travelled for two days. They moved ahead. As they approached near Chikmanglur town, Murali, suggested going to the local police station there. Inspector Swami, who was posted there, was an old friend of Murali.

Swami was delighted to see Murali after such a long time. As they informed him about their quest trailing an Ambulance, Swami interrupted them with urgency. He said "Wait! Wait, I got some information for you" The Duo jumped up and said "What? What do you know about the Ambulance?" Swami said, "I am not sure, whether it is connected, with the same ambulance, you are searching. Two days back the villagers, who went into the forest for collecting firewood, found a young woman dumped in the bushes and reported to the police. We found the lady, in her early twenties, badly bruised and unconscious. On admission to hospital, the doctor said that she was not injured seriously, but was unconscious due to the influence of some medication. This way we could not question her and we are waiting for her to come to consciousness. She definitely did not look as if she belonged to this region. She was wearing a blue Shirt, and faded blue jeans, and lot of fashion jewellery and appeared quite stylish. The label in her dress belonged to a shop in Mumbai. We had informed all police stations about any missing report, about a young lady, but so far......" Before he could finish his sentence, Murali and Rohit had already sprang to their feet and said, "Please, Swamy hurry and take us to the hospital immediately. We want to see this girl. It could be our officer"

As they walked the corridor of the hospital, the two young officers were filled with anxiety and apprehension, anticipating the worst. They walked briskly towards the special room. Just as they turned into the corridor of the room, they found a group of nurses and doctors having a hushed conversation. A grim situation brooded over all over their faces. Murali feared the worst.

The senior doctor noticed Swamy approaching and said "Sir, that injured lady whom we had admitted has vanished from the hospital." Murali and Rohit stood very still not knowing what to talk. Inspector Swamy said in a harsh tone "That lady was unconscious and we had kept a guard for the room. Then how could it have happened Doctor?"

The doctor said "Possibly, she came to consciousness some time back and was still pretending to be unconscious waiting for a chance. You know how our guards are! Seeing her very still, this man had just moved, for a cup of tea. By two minutes, he was back, with the teacup. The tea maker machine is just at this corner. But in those two minutes, this lady had got up, and made her escape. It is possible that she doesn't want the attacker to know that she is alive or she did not want to get involved in a police case or may be a criminal herself. But I say, this lady cannot be an ordinary lady. A normal girl cannot plan an escape so fast as this"

Swamy looked at the two and shrugged his shoulder. Murali sighed and said "Another dead end. Swamy, show us the spot at the slope of the mountain and let us see the place where this girl was found"

They drove to the site in the forest where the young girl was found. They had to stop their car, quite some distance away. They walked up to the bush and then came back to the spot, where they had left their car. They examined the spot carefully.

Swamy said, "Generally no vehicles come up to here. That day some villagers have seen vaguely a large vehicle going this way. They have seen only the back of that vehicle and hence are not sure if it was an ambulance. Probably it was the same ambulance you are looking for. Beyond this point, there is only thick jungle. Not even a path where you can walk" Murali nodded his head and stood thinking. Though smudged, half erased in the muddy patch, they could still see large tire marks that had crushed the grass on one side. There was no further way to go inside. That means they would have stopped the van here and carried the lady, walking into the bush, thrown her inside the bush. They must have thought that she is already dead and hence left her as it is. Murali wondered by any chance if Sherya was in that Ambulance at that time, why she did not use this opportunity, to escape into the jungle. It is possible that they had injured her so badly, that she was not in a position, to get up and escape. Then who is this injured lady? Or was this lady they carried and threw Sherya? If so then why she did not contact the local police when she got up? If this girl was someone else, another victim of their experiment in the nursing home, again why she did not seek help, from police?" Murali and Rohit got back into their car, and started going further in the path traced by the chip.

The base of the trekking camp happened to be on their way. They noticed that there were many people around and there was a lot of commotion. They got down and enquired. They heard that three young boys who went for trekking three days back were missing. They were told that the boys went with a team from this very base were lost on the way. Their guide spoke to Murali and Rohit. He said "Sir, for past fifteen years I am taking college children regularly for trekking. Not a single time, anything has happened, not even a minor injury. The route we trek is not through thick forest or slippery rocks. They are well-worn, well-known trekking routes. I have taken so many safety precautions and also, gave clear instructions and maps. I am totally at a loss to understand how the kids disappeared! Now I think with this, my camp has to be closed soon. No one would venture to come with us anymore"

Back in their car Rohit said "Murali is it possible that these boys by chance had come across the ambulance? They could have seen something odd and in their boyish immaturity tried to explore or dig something. The criminals could have caught them sneaking and got rid of them? What is your opinion?" Murali driving the car remained silent, for some time and said in a tired voice "Quite possible Rohit. The Ambulance had gone this way. The boys could have stumbled by accident in to it, and found something curious in there. These criminals can do anything." Rohit suddenly said "Murali, all this time we are looking and enquiring about the people in an ambulance. But suppose they have shifted vehicles? A lorry, a school bus, a car they could have used anything to travel and will not be too obvious on the road." Murali was completely irate and frustrated by now, "You are perfectly right. Anything is possible. We don't have a single clue except what we started out with, that our officer had travelled by this route, alive, but not necessarily conscious."

They finally travelled through the rough slope of the rugged mountain. The road was too narrow, and too rough, even for their small car. Finally, they could not drive any further. They parked and got out. They started walking on foot, stepping carefully through the hard rocks. After ten minutes of laborious climbing, they ended on a solid rock mountain. They stood there and looked around. Even if the ambulance or a small car or whatever they were driving, they could not have climbed beyond the point where Murali and Rohit had stopped the car. Then they could have reversed their car and gone away. If they know they cannot climb beyond this point, why should they climb up to this point at all? They tapped and examined the rock mountain with their hand for any hollow sound to see if there was any opening or cave behind it. They could find none. They walked back to the car. Before getting inside the car, Murali walked to the edge of the rock and peered at the steep, ominous looking, the deep valley. Rohit, understanding what his companion was looking for, stood along with him, and looked at what seemed like a bottomless abyss. It was a sheer vertical drop. Both the boys looked at each other. The same abject thought had crossed their minds.

Murali said, "If that lady was not Sherya then they must have climbed this high only to throw the injured officer in side this valley, where no one can get her body. That is the same reason, why the tracer worked up to this point and stopped." Rohit said, "It is a real bad news, for us to report. But we don't have any alternative."

They got into their car and carefully started reversing their car. When they reached a leveled area, Murali started turning his car. Rohit, struck with some sudden brain wave shouted "Stop Murali! Stop the car." He got out and Murali followed suit. Rohit started examining the sandy soil on the ground at this point. This well leveled area looked as a well-used spot and was big enough for any heavy vehicle. There were multiple tire marks all around in this area. Murali said, "These marks show that many vehicles have come up to this point and many times. But the question is why and for what purpose?' They walked up to the base of that mountain range and again scrutinized the steep rocks towering so high above them. There was a thick growth of bushes and trees at the base of the rocks.

Rohit said in a half-surprised voice "Murali did you notice this? As we climb up the hill, the vegetation was becoming thinner and thinner, ending up finally in thin grass. But at this point there is so much thick vegetation as if someone has carefully tended them with water and manure." Murali answered very casually, "You don't know Rohit that these valley is a part of western Ghats and are made up of volcanic rocks. It is possible that some pockets have more frozen lava and hence have rich manure for vegetation." Rohit laughed heartily and said "You are now talking like an expert Geologist" Murali replied calmly "Honestly, Rohit, I had taken geology as one of my subject in my B.Sc.! How do you think I got 95% in my B.Sc.?" Rohit looked back at him with surprise and after one second understood the joke as Murali burst out laughing. They walked back to their car and headed back towards Mumbai.

Chapter 22

The changeover

She fell into a disturbed sleep when a knock at the door, woke her up. She checked her watch. It was two thirty pm. She got up and opened the door. The driver's assistant stood there with a parcel, which was filled with aroma of food. He handed it out and said "Here is food for you sister. If you want water, it will be there in the fridge" She took the food and keeping it on the seat asked meekly "Could I use the bathroom?" He nodded his head, and helped her to get down. He walked ahead, and she followed him. He stopped, and pointed to the side of the hotel and went away. She stood there and looked around. They were parked in a narrow mud road away from the main road. There were coconut and palm trees all around. The soil was rich red. Tiny huts dotted along the mud road. A few tile roofed two storied houses stood proudly amidst them. She crushed the deep layer of her brain and searched through all her geography knowledge. They were in Karnataka for sure. Calculating approximately from the time they had travelled and the topography of this place, she guessed that they must be somewhere near or around Mangalore.

She walked towards the tiny hotel. It was just a small house, whose front room was fashioned in to a teashop. A she stood gazing around, an old woman came out of the house and gestured that she should follow her. From the ease and familiarity of the old lady's behaviour, she gathered that this may be a usual spot, where these people took a break every time. That meant that the Ambulance and medicine regularly travelled through this way, and this may be some regular, trusted jaunt. She followed the woman and entered the house. She passed through three dimly lit room, one after other. In the first room there were two men, and in other rooms there were some women. But none of them looked up or even threw a cursory glance at her. Thankfully, she reached the bathroom and the lady went back. She washed her face and as she looked up at the old smoked mirror, she was shocked to see the amount of bruises and cuts in her face, which were now turning into an angry purple blue. There was a knock at the door. She understood that the lady was standing right outside, all this time, guarding the door. She came out and without looking at the lady walked back very fast and stepped into the steps of the ambulance and locked the door.

Having come from outside, she suddenly noticed the difference in the temperature outside and inside and realized that the Ambulance was heavily air-conditioned. Why was the air conditioner running so high when there was no patient? There was no oxygen cylinder, or cardiogram machine or any other monitors generally seen in emergency ambulance. So, she reasoned, the air conditioning was not for the patient. She groped around in the semi darkness around the sides of the ambulance and found a light switch. She flipped it and now started a thorough inspection. She remembered what the man had said about water. He said Fridge! She tried to locate the fridge in the over packed ambulance. She wadded through the large parcels, reached the backside of the van and found a large sized fridge. She opened it and one moment stood spellbound. The fridge was packed to capacity, with various medicines and injections. She gathered that this Ambulance was not meant for carrying patients, but medicines regularly to certain destination. The ambulance was air conditioned for the safety of the medicines.

Like a sudden bolt of lightning, she suddenly realized the gravity of the situation. She was going to a totally unknown place, pretending to be a nurse, expected to take care of some important operation or patients. Her instincts warned her that she was soon going to be entering some central point of the criminal. She had to be very well prepared and not arouse any suspicion.

First she had to be equipped with the background knowledge of the nurse whose place she had managed to switch. She cast a sweeping glance all around and found a travel bag on the nurse's seat. She yanked it open in a hurry. Right on, the top of the neatly piled dress, there sat a thin folder with name AMMU written in bold letters. She picked it up with trembling fingers and focused her mind in to complete attention as she opened it. The first sheet was an appointment letter, printed on some strange letterhead. The letter head was not of any known language, but it was a strange coded language with some pictures and numbers at random. She looked at the typed letter. It was an appointment letter of a new nurse. It read that in place of the deceased nurse Kunjamma, her sister Ammu kutti Jhosep, would take up her duties. Next paper was a certificate. A nurse's diploma in the name Ammu kutti Joseph from Trisoor, Kerala. She flipped the next page. It was the bio-data of the said nurse with a photograph and her previous experience certificate. Her past experience was in a hospital for three years. She pored over the photograph carefully. The photograph was probably taken without enough light or was an old one. Ammu's image was a little dark and the features were hardly clear. But Ammu's height was five three according to her bio-data.! She found a ball point clipped on the side of the folder. She managed to round of the printed number 3 on the form, to an 8. Ammu had short cut hair. So that was good. If someone scrutinized the photograph very closely and compared her face they might still be able to spot the differences. An idea bubbled in her head. Actually, the bruises in her face could help her to draw the attention of the viewer and distract from the comparisons. She decided to make it look more prominent and looked around. The corner of the seat was covered with a thick layer of dust. She rubbed her hand on the dust. Then she painted her face liberally with that dark dust especially all around the bruised regions. She studied every thing about Ammu from the documents like her schooling the hospital she served, her family etc, and memorized the details. The bag contained some clothes and necessary materials. She zipped the bag and started waiting.

After about one hour of travel, the Ambulance started climbing up steeply. There were a series of sharp, violent jerks, and the body of the ambulance shuddered and quivered, like a man with malaria fever. The parcels skidded, from side to side and made cling-clang noises, as the glass bottles inside them jolted. She managed to balance herself by hanging on to the strap on the top of the seat. She suddenly noticed one of the windows, that had been hidden behind the tower of parcels, was now accessible. She quickly yanked the curtain of the ambulance. The Sun has just set, but still there was enough light to see things clearly. She found that the ambulance was climbing up the mountain, through a narrow valley. About half an hour, they climbed. Then, the ambulance made a sharp left turn and stopped for five minutes. She thought that they had reached their destination, and expected a knock on the door. Instead, she heard some strange, mechanical, grinding noise of some machinery. She wanted to look out, but the ambulance started moving ahead with a jerk. Then, it started to move very smoothly as if going on a good paved road. It was pitch dark suddenly and she could not see anything. After a few seconds, she could see a faint light again. She saw that they were going through a well-constructed underpass. It was dimly lit but illuminated at regular intervals. The van now rushed on in full speed. Fifteen minutes of travel and then the van came to the end of its long journey.

She could hear now hear many voices, brisk, strict orders being barked and distinct sounds of heavy boots. Then, there was a knock on the door. She straightened her nurse uniform and picking up the travel bag and reached the door. She opened it. Oh God! She exclaimed and stood stupefied. In all her years of police training, she was clearly not prepared for what she saw ahead.

Chapter 23

Ammu at the Hospital

Sherya had guessed Ammu was a nurse when she switched places with her in the van after that valiant fight, Sherya in her new avatar, knew that she would have to work in some capacity at the hospital destination. Still, as she swung open the Ambulance door, with a bag in her hand, she saw what looked like a top-secret military operation. A group of about five or six Army men stood facing her, beckoning her with an automatic gun. They were wearing typical battlefield uniforms, heavy boots, green cap, binoculars, phones slung in their belts and unmistakable state of the art automatic guns. One of them said in a rough, harsh commanding voice of army (army rules, only orders, no requests) "Get down fast"

She stumbled out quickly, without anybody's help this time. As they stood around, she felt so puny in front of them. Her own father was in Army as a colonel, and in the past, she had ample interaction with many Army men. But she had never seen a regiment, all so well built. All of them were at least six feet three inches height. They were equally broad shouldered and looked like giants. After one second, she realized that they were standing there to get into the ambulance and unload and not to scrutinize her. Seeing her, still standing there, one of them gestured with his gun impatiently "Move, there"

Ammu was still in a daze. An Army operation was the last thing on the earth she had expected. She had read that powerful countries like US, Russia etc engage in secret research for their Army, and some time even use common citizens as guinea pigs. Was our Army working hand in hand with some other country? What was this secret research? Seeing her still standing in the same spot, one solder yanked her hand roughly and pulled her to the side cabin. He said, "Go in and show your papers" She, recovering from her world of thoughts, walked a few steps, and reached a desk. A lady in same army uniform, sat there. She looked up and said "New nurse? Show me your papers!" She pulled the folder and gave it to her. As the lady skimmed through the folder, she watched her face. She prepared herself for any question that would arise from the differences in the photograph. But the lady just looked at the photo and gave her a cursory glance. She read the file again and snapped it close. Handing it back she said, "Go with him inside" She pointed to a solder, standing ready, a little further away. As she walked to him, he mouthed "MOVE"

He turned and started walking through a gate and entered a corridor. The corridor was dimly lit. Their footsteps echoed in eerily. The corridor was about eight feet wide and around ten feet high. The ground was covered with rough coir matting, and it was a little damp, due to some water oozing, from somewhere. Ammu noticed that strangely, all the lights were fixed at a lower height, at about three feet from ground, their shades facing down. The domes were painted black on the top. Thus, the vision was pretty much at ground level. She craned her neck, and tried to look up at the ceiling. She could see nothing. After a few seconds, when her eyes got used to the dull light, she could see hard, rough projecting rocks on the top. She guessed that they were under some rocky mountain slope or cave. The man walking ahead stopped, and shouted, "Move fast." She started walking fast without looking around.

It was very quiet all around, and their own footsteps were aggravating her throbbing headache. It seemed that they were waking endlessly. Actually, they had walked only about fifteen minutes. The man walking in the front, now stopped. They were, now, facing a dark olive colour painted door. There was no lock and he pushed it open. The door opened with a creaking noise, a sound of not wood, but of a tin material. Ammu made a mental note. Now they were in the main portion, an expansive lobby like space had opened up.

There was an unusual looking, large, a raised platform, raised about two feet, above the ground. A large semicircular desk was placed on that. It looked like the usual reception desk of the hospitals except for its height. Three women were busy at work there. The solder ordered, "Go in." And even before she stepped in, he had slammed the door behind him, as he left. She walked to the desk hesitantly. One of the lady looked up and pointed ahead and said "Go to that table" Now Ammu noticed that besides the platform, there was another single desk, and a lady solder, in uniform sat there. When Ammu reached the table the uniformed lady officer said "Sit down and show me your papers" She took the folder and studied the papers a little more deeply, carefully, reading every page. She removed the appointment letter from the clip of the folder and examined it against her table light. Ammu understood that she was checking for some watermark, or some secret inscription in the letter. Satisfied with the paperwork, she put it back, carefully in the clip, and now looked at the photograph. She turned to Ammu and said,

"Turn your face to the side" She calmed herself and did as she was asked. Then the officer asked sharply "Why there are so many bruises on your face?" Ammu started answering in a stammering voice, keeping her accent heavy, as if she was struggling to speak the language. She said "Madam, our Kerala, you know, rocky everywhere" She swallowed, to show her nervousness. "You know Madam, it becomes very slippery in rainy season. While walking to the station, I slipped and fell on my face. The rough ground scarred my face. Hope it will not leave many marks on my face." The lady seemed satisfied with this answer. Ammu thought that the typical way in which she talked, had made her seem like naïve and stupid.

The lady was scoffing and her intellectual level, exactly as she had thought. She kept Ammu's folder in her drawer and said, "This would remain with me hereafter." Ammu nodded. The lady opened another drawer and gave her a key and said "That is your locker. Go and have a shower first and wear our sterilized uniform." Next, she pulled a folder from another drawer and handing her the folder spoke very slowly, as if to help her understand, "Read this very very carefully. This is the code of conduct, rules and regulations, of this hospital. You have to strictly follow them. Remember that always." Then she beckoned ladies working on the main desk, and said "Sona, you take Ammu to locker, and show her the shower room." One of the girls got up from the desk. Sona said in a flat voice, absolutely without any emotion or feeling, "Ammu, Come with me" and started walking briskly ahead. Taking a few seconds to respond, she got a glare from Sona. "Ammu" Sherya repeated to herself. "I should be careful to react more instinctively to it" she said to herself.

Now they walked through the huge room. On the other end of the large room, inside, Ammu could see a line of cubicles separated by curtains. Nurses were walking around busily. The passage they were walking was separated from the main hall by transparent white plastic sheets. Sona stopped, and showed her a large set of storage lockers, and said, "Keep your bag inside the locker number 302 and lock it." When Ammu finished, she said "Give the keys back to me" Ammu was surprised. "I will need the clothes and other things. Why you want me to return the key?" Sona took the key from her and said, "All the needed things, from tooth brush to your comb, will be supplied here. You can take your bag back, only when you leave. Now come with me, and I will show you the shower room". Just then another lady nurse, walked in there and said, "Ammu, your Tea". She handed her the tea cup, and vanished, as fast as she appeared. A hot tea was most welcome. She gulped it fast. As she drank the tea, she noticed that Sona was looking at her face, with a strange expression.

Ammu stopped drinking and asked gently, "What happened Sona? Why are you looking at me like that?" Sona, whose face had momentarily looked interested in her, turned her face away quickly, and murmured "Just nothing" They walked further, and Sona pushed open the bathroom section. There were about two dozen bath cubicles. She entered one. A towel was ready there for her. Sona turned, and walked away, without saying a word. As she turned the shower on, Ammu found her sprits rising. Fresh blood gushed into her head. She was feeling really very, very happy, for no reason. She actually started humming a song and felt at the top of the world!

As she stepped out of the stainless steel bathroom stall, she saw a row of four sinks. Disposable new toothbrush was ready. An exact amount of toothpaste shot out of the dispenser and automatically stopped. Finally, a clean body after ages had refreshed her. She was feeling pleasant and happy. As she turned to look around for her uniform, another nurse was waiting ready there. She said, "Ammu, your dress is here. You will be keep them in this shelf hereafter". Ammu saw a big cupboard with open shelves. There were four sets of uniforms and undergarments, a comb and a single hair tie. Her shelf was numbered 302. She got into the uniform. It was a light blue coloured T- shirt and loose, elastic waist pant of the same colour. There was a plastic transparent, pocket attached to the front side of the shirt. No other pockets on the pant, she noted. Ammu dressed carefully. The uniform was loose. She understood that the uniforms were of standard size, and stitched in such a way that a heavy girl could also fit into it. The sister appeared again. She motioned her to come. Ammu followed.

Chapter 24

The elusive connections

The conference room was silent, shocked by the new information they had just heard. The Commissioner had just told the group two reports he had received from Delhi crime Branch head. One was the abduction of a group of nurses, and another of a group of young girls, from villages for a non-existing exhibition. The Delhi crime branch head had instructed the Mumbai crime office to work on these cases immediately. There was a serious possibility of this disappearance of large groups of women escalating in to a serious national issue.

The commissioner stared at the worried face of the group, and said, "You might remember, that sometime back itself, Jadav told us, that the case at the nursing home where Sherya disappeared was only a tip of the iceberg. I have to admit, I think he was very right. All these cases, in different places of India, yet all of them might be connected, to a larger ring of crime. We are still not able to identify any lead, or pinpoint the type of this crime that these criminals are engaged in. Secondly, who could be the mastermind and what is the motive?

Let us say, if we agree, that this is a human trafficking racket, then the murder of four girls, and abduction of young girls from village, all fall in place. Then we could say that the four girls could have be murdered because they could have resisted their abduction. But in the past, human trafficking has never been done openly like this, talking to the villagers, and then taking away the girls. What audacity! Then abduction was never done in a large number like this ever, at one shot, but in numbers of two or three, by luring the individual with job or marriage. Then if sixty or seventy girls are abducted, how did they manage to go out of India unnoticed?" Inspector Kurian said "Sir, they could not have gone by flight. Someone was bound to notice such a huge set of girls. So it is obvious, that they had to be smuggled by the illegal boats, to their destination. If we inform all our costal Naval officers, we would be able to catch them before they leave India" Commissioner replied in a tired voice,

"Kurian the pity is, that we are getting this information, very late. It is only because of an alert, sincere, NGO Director Dr Aruna, that at least now, we are getting this information. The girls had been taken away about eight months back and she came to know about them, only when she visited the village, a week back. The villagers have still not even realized that the girls are abducted. In fact there is no police complain so far."

There was another spell off silence. Then Jadav said "Even if we conclude that the girls were abducted for trafficking, it does not make any sense. Girls are generally taken away from North, from more interior parts, backward and underdeveloped villages, where the people are very ignorant. But not from places like Karnataka, where there was an elected Panchayat, and people were having at least, basic education, and were aware, of the world outside. Secondly what about the nurses? Why were the nurses abducted?" Somehow, there were only questions and no answers in the room that day.

Then the Commissioner called the two officers who were asked to travel in the same line tracked by the computer chip on Sherya's hand. Rohit and Murali reported about their findings. No one had heard, or seen any ambulance, nor that had it stopped for any tea or food. Secondly, they talked about the girl found in the forest, dressed in clothing from Mumbai, but who disappeared secretly. Thirdly they reported about the three missing boys from the trekking group. Finally, they talked about their climb till the end of the mountain. Gadre said "In short we have not got any leads from your tour. The girl, could be some isolated case of small time crime, and could have, ran away from police. The boys' disappearance could have been totally unconnected accident." He looked back at Jadav and asked, "What do you think Jadav?"

Jadav looked seriously worried as he replied, "Sir, On the other hand, I strongly feel that all these cases, might be linked. The lady found in the forest cannot be our officer, because she would have definitely contacted us, when she came back to consciousness. But definitely, she belongs to this picture, connected somewhere. Sherya's chip had shown movement up to the mountain range, and I believe she is still somewhere there, around that point, with or without the knowledge, of the criminals. Since we all know, that this crime operation is large scale, we have to attack this point on the mountain with a large backup force."

Everyone agreed to this, for the time being. Then the three officers, who had been working on collection of data about the mountains, put up their findings, with charts on the board. Kiran, one of the officer started explaining." Sir, this mountain ranges where our signal was sited last, belongs to this point." Pointing to that point he continued "This mountain range is one part of a twin mountain range. One of its base, is here and other base is near Banglore. Though they are the twin mountains, they are not exactly joined. Both of them are separated by a huge canyon.. but a dangerous vertical valley. The sides of the canyon are made up of practically vertical on either side. People do trekking the double mountain on either from Chikmangloor, or Banglore base, but no one had ever reached the valley as such. The slope of the mountain being so steep, dangerous, it is not possible even for the mountaineering people to know what is there below. It is said that since the rocks so hard and vertical, the climbers are not able to get any foothold nor can they hammer any footholds on them. Thick forest had covered one part of this region but most of the remaining canyon is made up dry, dead volcanic rock. It is impossible for any human being to get inside here or to set up a camp" Having finished his presentation, Kiran sat down. Gadre gave them an appreciative look and said, "Well done boys, Good study!" Turning towards Jadav he said "Now tell me, Jadav what is your plan? Now it is definite from the report of these boys that no one could camp in this mountain. You agree with that?" Jadav said

"Sir, I still firmly believe that there is something we are missing out here. If not in the canyon then camp might be set up inside the deep jungle. But it should be definitely there...…Deep in those mountains is my answer, Sir. To begin with tomorrow we would request the help of Air force personnel to make an aerial survey by planes, and take photographs of the valley and then we could plan our next move. That's all I can request now Sir"

Next day early morning, three Air force planes took off, to help the mission and they repeatedly circled over the jungle. The camera attached to the planes beamed clear images. The crime branch officers sitting in the conference room pored over these images in the monitor. Jadav talking on phone to the pilot, requested to move and scan some regions, repeatedly and the pilot obliged. Yet, in spite of their best efforts they could not penetrate through the dense forest. Finally, they had to abandon the scans and brainstorm some other strategy for the investigation. For Jadav, that night seemed especially dark. As time until daybreak stretched endlessly, his mind made up a million difficult situations Sherya could be trapped in.

Chapter 25

Ammu's patients

Ammu silently followed the nurse. They walked through a very long, long, vacant stretch of a room, stretching endlessly. She wondered in heart "What could be the use of this long vacant space in a hospital? Why is so much space wasted" She noticed that in all these places, all throughout the hospital, the lighting was still dim, with the black painted domes of light facing down, giving minimum light. After walking about twenty minutes she saw some empty beds lined up, about twenty-five of them, all empty. The nurse told her "These are the cots for us nurses, to sleep. That is, when we get off time". Finally, they reached a row of small spaces, cubicles created by curtains on all sides. The cubicles were on either side of a long walking path. Ammu, quickly estimated the numbers, twenty-five on each side. Each cubicle had a number plate. The curtains were kept drawn, and Ammu could not see the patients inside. They stopped at number 22, and the nurse opened the curtain of a cubicle. She said, "Ammu, your duty is here in this cubicle. You have to take care of these two patients" Ammu stepped inside the cubicle behind the nurse, and the sight of the patient, shocked her beyond words

She had expected that some special injured solders were being treated here in this hospital. Mentally, she was still playing out various scenarios for this covert operation by the Indian Army. But there were no soldiers there. There were two pregnant women in the two cots. Lot of monitors were attached to them, to continuously monitor, their vitals. She stood frozen, staring, when the nurse's voice awoke her. The nurse said, "Ammu, you have to be very alert, and be very careful, in watching these patients. They are very precious for us. Even if there is a slightest difference in the monitor reading, you should ring the alarm for the doctor. See this is the button?" She pointed to the red switch, near a wooden chair. The nurse added, "This is your seat. You are not to move out of the cubicle, not even a moment. If there is any need, use this intercom, for calling the reception. Every day, your duty will be switched to other cubicles of pregnant ladies" Without waiting for any questions, the nurse turned back, and pulling back the curtains and disappeared.

Ammu was still too dazed. Questions exploded in her head. Who are these pregnant women, seeming to be in a serious condition, needing so much medical attention.. why were they here..being treated by the Army? Is it possible that these women are wives of some criminals? No, It did not make any sense. Our Police would have kept them safe but in some proper hospital. Why this secrecy? Why this, isolation? Who are these ladies? Now, she started doubting these people outside in Army uniform..Could they not be the real Army, but terrorists disguised in uniform? If they are terrorists, is it possible that these women were hostages.....Some high level police or politician's wives? But, even assuming that they had abducted the women, how could be all the women be pregnant? Why would anyone specifically abduct pregnant women, who are difficult to look after? Then create such elaborate infrastructure to take care of them so earnestly?" There were a million question ...and no answers.

As she sat on the sole wooden chair, the chair wobbled and creaked. The chair was an upright, hard wooden chair without even a cushion. It also seemed a bit small even for her thin body. Cleary, the expectation was to sit upright and keep alert. If you slept off in spite of the uncomfortable chair, you would certainly fall off. Shreya had no intentions of sleeping. She got up and went near one of the patients. She leaned near the patient's face, smiled cheerfully, and said "Hello, Mam I am your nurse Ammu." She expected the patient to smile, and answer back. But the patient remained silent. She said once again, "Hello." The patients' face, which was so far indifferent, suddenly became hardened, turning red, her eyes, blazed with hatred, and she muttered, a curse in a muffled voice, and turned her face away. Ammu stood shocked, still unable to grasp anything.

She could understand that for some reason the patient were very upset and angry. She thought that may be due to their illness, and physical stress the patient was not cheerful. She now noticed, that the patient, surprisingly was very young, hardly seventeen! She turned, to the other patient in the room. The other patient was so far watching everything that was happening, between Ammu and the patient. As Ammu turned towards her, she hurriedly turned on her side, turning her back to Ammu and closed her eyes. Clearly, she did not want to be disturbed. Ammu went back to her chair. Her head was spinning.

What strange place and what strange people! That other girl was also very young looking, might be just sixteen years. About half an hour passed. A bell started ringing. A nurse from the neighbouring cabin peeped out and said, "You have to put the patients in the sitting position, and wait till the next bell"

Ammu moved near the bed. She studied the levers of the bed, and then shifted the first lady to a sitting position. She repeated the same with the next patient. The patients were facing each other now, but did not talk or even smile at each other. They seemed resentful or resigned. Ammu saw the charts hanging on their cots. Both the girls were pregnant with three babies each! Ammu nearly collapsed with shock. Two teenage pregnancies with triplets in one room, tucked away in entire secrecy!!

Dinner for the patient and nurse was served in the cubicle. She silently helped the patients to eat their dinner. The dinner was of very high standard, lot of protein, cheese, vegetables and fruits, while her meal was just two dry chapattis and a small serving of vegetable. Another woman in Military Uniform entered, checked the patients and gave injection and tablets to the patient. Ammu understood the fact. They were not taking any chances, by giving the charge of medication to the nurses. The patients went to sleep. Ammu's first day in the hospital had been smooth but completely flummoxing.

Chapter 26

The temple in the mountains

Fourteen months back.- --

Shivram Prohit was the local priest in a small temple near the base camp of the trekking school. The trekking group and their guides always came to the temple before they started their adventurous journey in the mountains. Vacation groups who come for site seeing also used to come there as it was the only temple of the forest goddess in that area. Shiva often wished that he could be a head priest in a big temple. He had only heard of large sums of donations and income from visitors. One fine day, his dream came true.

A foreigner had come looking for him. He said he was Jhon from America. He narrated his sad story to Shivram. Jhon had come to India on his office job and fallen head over heels in love with a Hindu girl, Leela from Mysore. They were both nature lovers and camped and trekked often. They lived happily for two years, when Leela suddenly was diagnosed with a rare cancer in its last stages. Before her death, she had expressed a rather weird wish to Jhon. She wanted him to build a white temple, on the top of a mountain in her memory. Jhon had been gone to many places, but in devout India, there was already a temple on every mountain peak! Hence he came to Chikmangloore, where many people go on trekking on the twin mountains, but there are no temples on the top. He asked Shiva to help him to build the temple. In return, Shiva could become the chief priest there. He wished to construct a small but exquisite temple on the peak, up to which people can trek. He wanted Shivram's help in the construction of the temple as he had no knowledge of the scriptures and requirements for the temple. Shivram's happiness knew no bounds, as Jhon gave him a thick wad of currency notes as advance for his help.

Shivram's family had been serving the forest goddess for generations now. He was well known to the locals. He took the Jhon, to the municipal authority, and forest official etc, and one by one, got clearance for the construction of the temple. The officials had initially said that the land belonged to forest area and no major construction could be allowed. But Shivram pushed the idea saying it was bound to be a very small structure, built on a single man's funds Jhon, a mark of love..They should allow it. The official then relented, allowing construction without any disturbance to the surrounding. With this condition, the letter of permission was granted and signed. Jhon also asked for permission for a minimum amount of electric supply, which would be drawn, from the power house at the Chikmanglore base, to light the temple and road leading to it.

The officer in charge of the power house looked at the request letter. An American building a temple for his Hindu wife! Why this could be the next Tajmahal he thought. The permission for the electric connection was given on a deposit of 50 lacks as security. Other officials from the municipal authorities had already given permission for land etc. Hence, he gave his approval, with a condition. The temple had to pay double the charge, for the current consumption, every month. All conditions were agreed and the letter for the permission was granted. Shivram was requested to get a team of his men to help in the construction, which further delighted him. He selected about thirty men from his own village.

Materials started coming in big vans. The workers, who were paid double wages, moved them to the top of the hill. A huge pile of ready to assemble cork boards, large size tarpaulins, thousands of bundles of sheets, ready to assemble tin doors, steel walls, and a million other things. As the goods were all dismantled and well packed in boxes, the workers lifting the loads did not have any hint of what they were carrying. In the quiet village, this was good income and no one bothered. The officers who had sanctioned the temple did not visit the site either.

Slowly huge rubber ducts were laid all the way, from the power station, to the top the mountain. One day, Shivram asked Jhon, about the need of the bulging ducts for simple electrical connections to light a small temple. Shivram had studied up to the Junior college level and was a bit more aware than the average villager. Jhon explained that the electric wire insulation of normal simple wires, might wear off in the heavy mountain rain. They could become dangerous for the people who move on the mountain for trekking. Hence, as a precaution the big ducts were being used to cover the insulated wires. Shivram was satisfied but was becoming acutely aware of the significant sum of money invested in this project.

All the materials had now reached the top of mountain. Particular care had been taken to cause no loud construction noise. A number of foreigners had now joined the group to lift the things. After five months the workers were paid. Shivram was in charge of paying wages and he made a handsome sum for himself. Now he was eager to see the progress of the temple. One fine morning, he started climbing. The trek as expected took him two days and he reached the peak. It was the said spot, which was much beyond the point, to which the trekkers would climb to. He was shocked to see an empty, dry patch of land staring at him at the supposed temple site. It was as it is, as he had seen it ten months back, without even a single brick!

He looked for the piles of material, moved up meticulously for so many days. All had vanished in thin air. The electric duct, which was supposed to be the current connection to the temple, was now connected to a huge transformer, whose output seemed to vanish into the mountain. There seemed to be huge holes drilled into the mountain. There was not a single foreigner or worker, or any one in the site now. Alarm bells started ringing in his brain. A foreigner, coming and asking for permission for a temple!! Why was so much materials brought in for a tiny temple? What is the need for this huge transformer? And where is the huge power generated, led into the mountain finally go? He looked at the ground, and found dried grass, showing a worn out path, made by a number of people walking. He followed the track. The track ended in a solid rock wall. There was no sign of steps going up or down. What had he done?

He decided to go and report it to the municipal commissioner. He started hurriedly walking back through the trekking path. He would have barely walked for five minutes, when he heard his name being called. He turned towards the voice and saw, his friend, Jhon standing at the top, and waving at him. He said "Shivram come here. This is the place of the temple" Shivram climbed back again, and walked towards the place where Jhon stood, which was about 100 mts away, from the original temple spot. As he reached the spot, he started firing questions breathlessly. He asked "Where is my temple? Where are the people and where are the materials?" The Jhon smiled and said," Shivram, you have forgotten the chosen spot and is now looking, at the wrong spot. We have already constructed, the temple on that said spot and all our men are still working there. Come with me. I will show you" He turned and started climbing, the steep hill and Shivram followed and started climbing. They climbed higher and higher. Shivram now half wondered if he had really missed the spot! How could temple be built this steep section?" Jhon now stopped, and pointed to slope on the other side and said "Look there. That is the temple. See how beautiful it is. My Leela will be happy no." Shivram smiled and moved one more step ahead to look down at the pointed place. Suddenly, he started falling, as he felt a hand shove him hard from the back. For a few seconds, his scream echoed among the various peaks of the mountain, as he dropped head along..then there was silence again. Jhon peered down again, having made sure that Shivram had gone down the valley, quietly started walking towards the rock wall.

Chapter 27

A break

It was the second day in the hospital for Ammu, four days since she was abducted from the nursing home. Early morning alarm rang. It was followed by the arrival of milk for the patients and tea for her. This was the only sign that another day has dawned. There was no trace of sunlight anywhere, and the hospital remained the same, as she had seen it, the previous night. In spite of the hard, rough chair, she had managed to get a few winks, because of her police training. She was wide awake now. She knew that there is no use in asking any one about the daylight. She pulled the patients to sitting position, and gave them the milk. She sat on her chair and started sipping her tea. It was piping hot and a delicious tea! Just one sip raised her mood, and suddenly she was feeling very happy! As she was about to take her second sip, she felt the eyes of the two patients looking straight at her. She looked up. They were looking at her with a strange expression, and a half suppressed smile. She looked at their faces, from one to another, and the moment they saw her eyes, they turned their faces away. Ammu passed a moment, and stopped drinking. These angry pregnant girls-- what was making them feel so amused now? Suddenly, a flash of memory occurred. She remembered how the nurse, who brought her tea yesterday, was also staring at her with a strange expression! Then she also recalled, the sudden blood gushing into her blood, and how she started, even humming a tune in the bath Now, she very slowly sipped one small spoon of tea, and kept it in her mouth without swallowing, as long as possible. The delicious flavour of sugar and spices, and finally a bitter taste hit her tongue. Oh God! The tea was drugged. Now she understood the meaning of the stare of the patients. They were watching her. They knew that the tea was drugged. She turned her back on the patients, and slowly walked up and down the room, pretending to drink. Finally she went near the sink and pretending to wash her cup, she quickly poured the tea down the sink, and put the empty cup on the tray.

She started thinking seriously. Why was her tea drugged? Is it because she is new and she should not show any resistance to any activity? Or is it possible that the tea was supposed to make all nurse's brain dull, and they worked like robots, for long hours, without getting tired? Surely they won't drug the patients, because that would hamper their pregnancy. She decided to remain more alert, about everything served for her.

Another bell started ringing. Ammu looked at her watch. It was nine AM though the room looked still dark. Another nurse entered and told her "Ammu bring the patient for sun light" She wheeled away one of her patient and Ammu started pushing, the wheel chair of another patient. They walked about ten minutes and reached the long open space. It was the same empty space, about which her brain was restlessly questioning. All fifty-eight women, pregnant with twins or triplets, were now in that spot. There was a mechanical noise, of a shutter rolling, and suddenly the room was filled with bright sunshine. At the sudden flash of sunlight, her eye winced, by reflex action. She looked up. She could see the blue sky, stretching on and on, high above them. A large tarpaulin which was covering the room had, now rolled back to a side to expose the sky. Now the patients were made to get up and walk in the sunlight up and down. "Sun bath for the patient" Ammu thought. The exercise went on for one hour. Then the top of the room was covered again, and the patients were made to go back to their bed. Ammu thought "This is one spot through which one can escape. But the tarpaulin was too high to reach" But all the same she made a mental note of it.

There was another break when the nurses were allowed to go for shower. Ammu saw about fifteen nurses there. However, not one of them talked a single word or exchanged even a smile. Ammu spotted a very young, very cheerful, looking nurse. Ammu went close to her and whispered, "Why no one is talking here?" The girl looked at her, and went back without answering. She went near the mirror, on the wall. The mirror was totally fogged up, by the steam from the showers. The nurse put her finger and started writing. "because we are being monitored" As Ammu looked at her bewildered, she nurse pointed to the wall. It was then that Ammu noticed that there were speakers attached, all over the bathroom walls. Even if the nurse whispered it would be heard. Ammu shrugged her shoulders, and the young nurse smiled warmly. Finally she had broken the ice with one nurse!

Chapter 28

The Aerial Survey

The meeting in the commissioner's conference room began. The commissioner Mr.. Gadre said, "Jadav we have done everything possible. It is five days since the officer has disappeared. If the den of the criminals is among the forest, as you suspect, then we are not able to get any clue from the aerial survey. Shall we send a team on foot, to comb that region?" Jadav said "Sir, I am sure that the den is definitely in this, unapproachable valley. Shreya's last signal was received from the mountain slope. So I suggest that somehow we have to reach that area in the valley"

Gadre said, "Jadav that valley is impossible to approach. According to our knowledge gathered so far, it is not just one criminal, but a whole group of criminals, are staying there. How can they camp there? They have also abducted nearly 50 to 55 females besides our officer. How is it possible to transport so many females into this valley? On our request, forest officers from Mysore had checked every inch of the mountain, once again, to see if there are any caves etc and they had found none. So what do you feel that we should do now?"

Jadav said, "Sir, sitting here in Mumbai, so for away, from the suspected site cannot help us. Our team should shift our base, to the nearest place, from this mountain. Then with the cooperation of the Air force unit there, we would survey the valley again"

Mr. Gadre said "Moving nearer to the point of crime is a good idea. Your entire team here can go to Mysore by flight, today itself. But even if you send helicopters for search, they cannot fly deep down, for the fear of getting knocked off by the ridges".

Jadav said, "Sir, first let us all move to day, and we would keep you informed about our progress". By four 'o' clock they all arrived Mysore, by a special plane. From there they proceeded by road to the base of the mountain.

They met the officials, whom Mr. Gadre had requested for help them. Jadav said "Sir, I would request you to give me a specially trained pilot who can successfully fly between the mountain range, and go down as deep as possible" By half an hour, the specialist pilot Nanda arrived at the meeting room. Jadav showed him the map, and described the area, he wanted to comb. Pilot Nanda looked at the map carefully. Looking up at Jadav he said "Sir it already nearing five 'o' clock. By the time we go to the Air base, and then move to this area, it would become dark. First it is risky to fly between the mountain in the dark, and the same time we won't be able to see anything once it becomes dark". Jadav said "Mr.. Nanda, I surely believe, that we would see something in the dark, than in the day time, provided you don't have any objection"

Nanda smiled and said "When a committed officer like you, is here, it becomes my duty to oblige" Nanda and Jadav got into the car for the Air base. Soon they were circling, over the valley in their helicopter. Jadav had night vision camera, and scanned every inch of the visible area.

Nanda said "Actually there is not much forest region here. We can fly even lower here. He dropped the height of the helicopter, and they circled. As they moved they found, that valley was totally dry devoid of any vegetation. There were only boulders and rocks. As they moved deeper they saw a water fall. The water fall was quite huge and large volumes of water, jumped over the rocky terrain below. Now they saw a thick growth of trees. It appeared so suddenly, that it looked as if they had gone to a totally different place! It was so thick, and green, that an inch of ground was not seen between them. Now it had become totally dark.

Nanda said, "Mr.. Jadav there is no camp here. In fact no trace, of any human being. It is getting very dark, and I feel that we should go back"

A disappointed Jadav, nodded his head and said "Yes I guess we have to go back" As the helicopter turned back, Nanda said "Very surprising, one half of the valley is so dry and rocky, and then suddenly there is such lush green trees on the other half.?"

Looking at Jadav's worried face, he said, "Mr. Jadav if you need, we can take another aerial survey tomorrow. By the way we have attached a powerful camera to the helicopter. In the night you may study them, and who knows you may get some clue "The helicopter returned to base. The entire team along with four more officers from local crime branch sat in the projection room. In the big screen the images recorded by the camera were projected, in a slow motion, so that every inch, could be seen clearly. With eyes like hawk, every pair of eyes watched. Everyone was dying, for some breaking point. After thirty minutes of watching, the camera came to last one minute when the helicopter started turning.

Jadav, spotted something, and said, "Stop, stop here" The image was frozen at that point.. Jadav said, "Zoom that point, the point on the right" The operator moved the curser, to the said point and zoomed. All could now see a tiny, sparkle of light, among the dense dark image of the forest. As they watched, it flickered and appeared again.

Jadav burst out, "There it is, see there is a light there below the forest trees. Probably they had carefully covered all the lights but by some chance the light from one source has escaped. This proves, that there is a camp there, very much there, but very efficiently, camouflaged" Every one clapped in happiness. Though they hardly know, how to enter the camp, in that deep valley, at least, they have some hope now, for the time being, and they were happy.

Chapter 29

The scientists in the mountain

Nine months back.

It was nearly three months, since Dr. Baskar Raju and his team of scientists moved with the military secret service officer. For the past three months they all had worked, very hard, and accomplished whatever Tippu Chinnaiya asked them to do. Dr. Bhaskar, guided his team very efficiently, and all work was finished before the dead line. Today as usual they were busy when Tippu entered, his military boots announcing his arrival loud in the room. "Hello, Dr. Raju, how is the work going on?" he asked.

Dr Raju pretended to smile and said "Yes Sir, we are working extra hours and had succeeded in the modification of the DNA as per your choice. So I presume that our job here is over and soon we can go back?"

Tippu laughed loudly, "Oh No! Not so soon doctor. Today we have got another set of eggs, and I would want you to work on this, and finish by ten days" He turned, and signaled to a military solder, standing behind him and said "Give the liquid nitrogen flask carefully to Dr Raju" The solder brought eight large flasks two at a time and kept them on the table.

Tippu said,"We had preserved the eggs in liquid Nitrogen in the frozen condition for the past three months. Please work on the alteration carefully, as you know this is a very important project for our military" Dr. Raju did not say anything but asked his assistant doctors to shift the flasks to the corner table. Tippu walked away.

There was a silence in the room. One of the young doctors asked in a soft whisper, "Sir, how long we are going to be captive like this? There is no solution to this?" Dr. Raju looked at the young faces and answered in a hoarse whisper "It was my greatest mistake, to get fooled by Tippu, believing that he was the real military officer. Now since we are caught in this mess, we are left with no other choice, but to pretend to be carrying on some work. I hope sooner or later.............."

He stopped his sentence and looked around the various video cameras kept all around the ceiling, of the work place. He walked to the table and pulled a paper and wrote something very fast, and showed it to all the young doctors and said "This is new system we are going to work on" The doctors read the message written on the paper. It read "Sooner or later our police, will definitely come and rescue us. By this time, they would have known that we are missing". The doctors shook their heads, and saying, "Yes Sir, we will do that" and walked back to their work.

Dr. Bhaskar Raju sat on his chair and closed his eyes. He remembered the day three months back when he and his team started with heart full of dreams. They left Banglore at five thirty am, early morning, and travelled by road for two days. But the last phase of their journey, which was for five hours, they could hardly remember the way they were travelling. They were feeling unusually sleepy after their tea at five pm. They had all woken up only, when they were shaken and asked to get down from the bus. The fist sight of their lab was not so thrilling. It was large military tent, with office on one side, and eleven cubicles for them to stay. Dr. Raju's first step was to go near the office table, and look at the super special microscopes, analysis machines, huge bottles of liquid nitrogen and other needed equipments. There were a number of computers and accessories.

As he was examining them Tippu said, "Dr. Bhaskar, we had nearly provided this lab, with all the laboratory equipments. Still if anything is needed, it would be provided it to you immediately. He then turned to the young doctors, and said "You have full AC room for research, separate cubicles for your rest. As this military project is highly confidential, none of you are allowed to use cell phone, e mail, or camera. The use of these computers, are restricted for getting as many data as you want, from internet. But you cannot send any data, or e mail outside for security reasons" Finishing his talk he walked away. The cubicles for their stay were comfortable. There was TV in some cubicles. But they could see only some local cable channel of movies, and music. There was no news channel. Good meals were provided. There were Tea and Coffee making machines at the work place. But by three days, the doctors started feeling suffocated. That day when Tippu visited them, as his usual rounds, the doctors requested for permission, to go out get some fresh air after their working hours.

Tippu was silent for some time and said in a reluctant voice "You doctors are suppose to work till eight in the night. Then when can you go out?" Dr. Raju said "Mr. Tippu, when the doctors work continuously under microscope, with their heads in the glass cubicles, sometime they do need, some fresh natural air" Tippu said "OK then, but while going out, all of you should go out as a group, and one of our solder will escort you so that you don't lose your way"

Next day evening under the pretext of fresh air they all went out from the camp tent. The solder walked them to about one Kilometer. The ground was all rocky and when they looked up the sky was so far away. High, steep mountain ranges ran on both the side. Finally, they reached a waterfall. The fresh sound of water gushing down, temporarily gave them a sense of relief. Dr. Raju said to the soldier, "We want to sit here for some time"

The solder said, "Yes I will wait here. I am sure, that, none of you smoke. Lighting a match is prohibited here. In fact, you cannot use torch light also to see the ground. So you people move before it gets very dark" Dr. Raju understood that they were trapped in a camp in a deep valley. Even if they wanted to escape, no one could climb the steep mountain range. At the other end, the water fall blocked the way.

Dr. Raju noticed that some type of crude hydraulic power generator was installed at the waterfall, to collect electricity. Besides this, a large number of generators, working on diesel oil, thundered, producing the current supply needed for the tents. Large water duct pipes were installed, which collected water from a filtration tank, and were then carrying the water into the tents. He also noticed that though the ground all around was dry, filled with hard rock and sand but the top of their camp tents looked lush green with vegetation. First he was confused at the contrast and the impossible growth. His intelligent brain soon discovered that they were not real growth, but were created artificially with number of cut out branches of trees and a number of artificial wines and flowers. He did not know that it was this green camouflage which preventing the discovery of the terrorist camp whenever the police did an aerial survey.

Dr. Raju just stood looking at all this and wondered about the marvel of work these terrorists had done for achieving their end. Finally, they all got up and walked back silently and the guard with the gun followed them.

Chapter 30

Dr. Gokul

It was time for the Doctor's rounds. Ammu had noticed that beyond the fifty cubicles for the patients, there was a large tent, which was shared by the seven doctors who took care of the patients. Today Ammu was in a new cubicle with new patients. This time she was wise, not to try to communicate with the patient. A doctor entered. He was thin built, short and looked around fifty plus. He wore large-framed ill-fitting spectacles. He started examining the patient. His voice was sharp and brusque as he talked to the patient.

Ammu saw that the patient was slow and not reacting to the doctor's instructions to move. She moved closer to the doctor, gave him a bright smile and said, "Sir, please let me help" She was shocked, as he quickly turned and hissed roughly "Sister you mind your own work. I can manage my work!" Ammu stepped back. In two days, she had moved five cubicles, and had met four doctors so far, three of them were very young. Still her charms and efforts at trying to make communication did not work. They all behaved the same way. Ammu wondered what she could do to strike a friendship here? She needed to get some information at least. Three full days had gone by here in hospital, wasted. She could not break the ice with any patient, or with her co nurses, or any other person. She had hoped that the doctors would catch on to her clues fast. Even if she had a chance to talk one single sentence, she could try to plan something. But unfortunately, all the doctors were as irritated as the patients. It felt like everyone was resentful and being held captive there. Just as she was pondering, one of the young patients suddenly started moaning and shivering. Ammu quickly pressed the red buzzer, and within two minutes, another young doctor and a staff sister in military uniform, arrived. Doctor for a change, had a cheerful face, talked kindly and soothingly to the patient and injected the patient. The patient slowly calmed down. The uniformed sister left the cubicle. Doctor still stood there, watching his patient. Ammu quickly decided to take a plunge with this doctor.

She smiled and said "Doctor, I am Ammu, new here, I have jointed in place of my sister Kunjamma" Doctor turned and looked at her, a bit surprised. He smiled back and said "I am doctor Gokul".

Ammu was elated. She came close to him and pretending to adjust the blanket whispered "Doctor I would need your help" She was facing the blanket, adjusting its fold and her voice was almost inaudible. Gokul, was silent for a second, and then suddenly, he raised his voice and exploded "Sister! Why are you so damn slow! Move please. I will do it myself".

As Ammu looked up stunned with his sudden behaviour he moved closer to her, his shoulders almost rubbing hers and whispered in her ears "Watch out! Video cameras up" He moved away quickly, took his prescription pad, and scribbled something. Handing it to her, he said "Be very careful, and watch the patient. If there is any problem, get these medicines from the military nurse" He briskly walked away. Ammu slowly lifted her head, and looked up. There were two tiny video cameras focused on the patients from two angles. She felt a little foolish that she had not noticed it earlier. Then she understood the attitude of all the doctors. She opened the folded prescription and looked. There was a message there "Ammu we are being watched all the time. Don't risk your life like your sister. She was shot dead. In case of emergency, write in a prescription pad and give me." Ammu looked at the patients. They were not paying any attention to her. She crushed the letter in her palm and after five minutes flushed it down the sink. A very tiny flicker of hope surged into her heart. Now she had a team of two friends, one nurse and one doctor Gokul.

At tea break she went to the reception desk and asked for a prescription pad and pen. Sister Sona, looked up and said "Ammu prescription pad is not given to the nurses. Only doctors are permitted to do so" Ammu said in a pleading voice "But some time the doctors give instruction so fast, and you know, I am new and I get nervous" Sona looked all around carefully, and thrust a paper pad with pen, below the desk and whispered "Take it and keep it hidden". Ammu crouched down near the floor. Pretending to adjust her shoes, she pulled the note pad and hid it under her shirt. After walking back some distance, she looked back. Sona was looking at her still. A very tiny glint of smile flickered in her eyes. One more friend added!

As she walked back, she saw the two military solders, repairing a broken lamp shade. They fitted it tightly and checked that no light leaked from the top. The staff nurse, supervising them, yelled in anger "How could you be so careless? What do you people do, in your night duty rounds? I only pray, that dome of the lamp had broken only today, and we had repaired it immediately"

Ammu stopped and looked at the light. She thought "Why Jadav Sir has not responded to my wrist signal? If they had done aerial survey in the night, they might not be able to spot anything because these lights are planted too low. But if they survey during the day, can't they spot the tent? What is going on there in the outside world? How long it would be, before I could communicate with Jadav Sir?" She was not aware that the radar on the tent cut off her signals from wrist. But she would have definitely felt happy, if she had known, that the same dome of the light had actually broken, two days ago itself! It had missed the guard's attention, and Jadav sir, had spotted that tiny light, in his aerial survey in the night.

Chapter 31

The butcher shop

It was a tiny butcher shop, in the small gullies, of Delhi. An old man, with a white, long, matted beard, continuously chopped red meat. He stopped working, as a continuous irritating cough caught his breath. He dropped his chopping knife on the table, and holding his sides with both his hand coughed on. A man passing by on the road said, with kindness "Gaffar Baba, take some break! At this age you need not work so hard"

Gaffar Baba, looked up and said "Thank you sir, for your kind words" Panting he sat on a small stool. A hefty built Khan entered the shop and said "Baba it is time we close the shop" Baba looked up. Their eyes met, and remained locked, for a second.

"Ok" He said "We can close the shop. You deliver this meat, to the hotel and come back. I will wait till, you come back" He walked to the wooden bench, on the back of the shop, and sat. Khan packed all the meat in a bag neatly. He then cleaned the table neatly with soap scrub. Taking the packed bag he left. After half an hour, he came back. He woke up Baba, and holding his hand, stepped out of the shop. They closed the shop, and got into the waiting auto. There was a pan- shop just in front of the meet shop.

Bansilal was making sweet pans, to his customers and he said, "Baba is nearly eighty. Still he works so hard" The customer was too happy to talk and he said "You know him for long?" Bansilal showed all his pan stained, yellow teeth, and said "Both of our shops are here, for not less than fifty years. Everyone around here knows Baba. He has no family of his own. But he works so hard, only to spend all that money, for any needy person. And he never looks about the community of the person, he helps. Actually he is paying the school fees for a dozen Christian children every month". The customer took the pan and said "Really amazing man"

The auto rickshaw moved through the mesh of small lanes, and finally reached the small Jugi of Baba. Khan helped Baba, to get down and both went inside the hut. Baba spread his mat on the ground and booth of them silently prayed. Finishing their prayers they had their dinner quietly. As Khan collected the empty plate he said "Baba, a demand had come. We have to make a contact today itself, so that the preparations can start"

Baba just nodded. They sat calmly, listening to music, from their radio, till ten thirty in the night. Now, Khan got up and closed the door, latched it and pulled the curtain over it. He walked to the back side wall, of the long hut. An old worn out carpet covered the floor. He rolled it. There as a wooden trap door. He opened it and waited. Baba got up and walked to the trap door. Both of them started going down the staircase. The last step ended in a wooden door. Khan carefully looked through the small view hole, and ascertaining, that the street is vacant, opened the door. They both stepped out in the dark street, and walked fast. They walked quickly, through the narrow, dirty, deserted lane, till they reached an old building. Baba knocked softly. The door opened. They entered and the room closed.

Miles away the cell phone of the young man tinkled softly. He picked up and said "Yes Baba, tell me." He listened for some time, and said "From Nepal? Baba, you know that there is, a so called bio- code, for every record. It won't be so easy like old days! And getting about fifty at one shot is just impossible"

Baba's voice answered, and it had a razor's cutting edge. "I know it is difficult. That is why my beta, you are there for me! Hire someone new, if need, but see that thing are done by one month. We had identified a new spot in Lucknow. Work has to start. OK Will talk latter"

The phone went dead. The young man sat very still thinking. The enormity of the job, and the risk and peril associated with it, send a chill down his spine. He paced up and down the room for some time and finally sat on his laptop. After five minutes he was chatting to his man with code name log head, about the needed hacking of the system.

Chapter 32

One more tent

It was the fifth night for Ammu in the strange so called hospital and she got her first night off. During the four days duty, she managed to peep into various cubicles, every possible corners she could manage. But she could make out nothing and there was absolutely no progress. Dr. Gokul did not come for anymore rounds. Except the one sweet baby nurse (she wished she had asked her name) she could manage to break the ice with two more nurses. But all the nurses were too scared, and she did not dare to talk anything to them. She was eagerly, looking forward for this night, to make some progress. The night shift nurse came at nine thirty to relieve her. Ammu handed over charges to her, and walked to her resting area. Five, six cots were already occupied, and the occupants were already fast asleep. She crossed through the full row of cots, and reached the last cot, in the line. She threw herself in the cot, and pulled the blanket all over her head, and waited. By twenty minutes, all the other sisters, who had night off, came, one by one. Ammu heard the soft footsteps, the ruffling of blankets, the cracking sound of old cots, and then finally, silence. One of the sister, had put off the light, and the sleeping area was totally in darkness. Ammu gently pushed her blanket, from one of eye and looked. She found the sweet baby nurse sleeping, in the next cot to her left. As she intently looked at her, Baby (Ammu had decided to call this nurse as baby) moved her eyes, and winked once. Ammu gathered baby was awake, and was watching her. Ammu thought that this can be an advantage, for her. She piled the pillows to the middle of the bed, and tucked the blanket all around the bulge. She rolled down from the cot. Rolling once again, she reached, the baby's cot, and whispered softly "Cover me if needed. I am going to be in the washroom with a bad stomach" Baby stretched her hand out, and gently touched the face of Ammu and said "Please take care"

For past three nights Ammu had made a detail study of the night settings. The reception and the next table of military nurse, all remained vacant in the night. The military solders, did not guard at the door. She first wanted to explore, the outside. She threw herself on the floor flat on her stomach and started crawling, very, very slowly like a caterpillar. One step, wait, watch, and move again. It was very dark, no human soul around, but still, she did not want, to take any chance. After five minutes of painful crawling, she reached the wall of the room. Thick black curtains, hung over the wall. She crawled under the curtain. There was about one foot distance between the actual wall and curtain. Ammu now sat up, took a deep breath, and now crawled on her knees, through the gap between the wall and curtain. She felt the wall with her fingers and found, that the wall was not a brick wall, but was made up of a ready to assemble planks, made of cork wood. She reached the end of the room, and now she was behind the curtain near the opening. She was next to the door, which leads to outside. It was again the same type of tin door, like the one she entered on her first night, but not the same door. She gingerly pushed the door, expecting a locked door. But to her surprise, it was just closed. Pushing it gently open, she crawled out. Now she was in the open and she prepared herself for whatever she is going to face. Once again she sprawled and flattened herself against the floor and looked around without raising her head. Surprisingly again there were no solders anywhere to be seen from this point. She craned her neck and looked up. The sky was clear with a crescent moon and stars. But the sky looked very, very far away. In the mild moon light she saw the huge tall mountain hills raising high against the sky. It was the same, on the other side. For the first time she realized, that they were captive inside some deep valley from where no one can escape. Even if helicopters are pushed in for service, how can so many, that also pregnant girls, be rescued? As her eyes moved to the ground level, she was more shocked, than surprised, to see another tent, just ten meters away.

She thought "Oh. God! Is it another tent of pregnant girls? Another fifty six, victims? But then, why the sisters, from our tent never got duty here?" This tenet is something different. She decided to find out. Since no one was around, taking a risk, she got up and hunching her body, ran through the distance, with a lightning speed. Reaching the tent, she went down on her knees, and pushed the tin door gently. Yes! This door was also not locked. It was pitch dark inside. She now went down to her caterpillar position again and started crawling inch by inch. As her eyes got adjusted to the darkness she could see about ten cubicles inside but all were drenched in darkness. When a patient is in the room it is never made totally dark. If there are no patients there, then who is there in these cubicles? Abruptly she stopped moving and thought of a plan in case she is caught! She decided that these must be the solder's resting place, and this moment the solders might be asleep there. In her restless head, again a question popped up. Generally the solders live only in the where all the cots will be lined up under one roof. No luxury of cubicles! That brings back the question again, as to what are these cubicles meant for and who are living there? As she waited pondering, to go ahead, or turn back, she felt a sudden chill on her spine. The training given for the police makes them have, sixth and seventh sense. Even in pitch darkness, in a quite still place, they can feel the presence, of another person. Now she felt, that, there are men there!. Not just one, but may be ten or eleven! They were sitting very quite there, just watching her, and holding their breath. If they were solders, they would have pounced on her. If they were nurses, they would have put on the light, and questioned her! Then who are these men, who are sitting so silently, watching her every move? She decided to take a plunge. She would make a move and see what happens!

But before she made her move, three pairs of hands grabbed her, and dragged her roughly. She was pinned down, totally. Someone held her hands tightly down and others were holding her legs down. From the darkness a voice questioned her with authority, "Who are you? What are you doing here in this night? If you have come here to steal our property you are not going back alive"

Ammu had enough strength, and potential, to knock off all their holds kick them off and fight. But the question asked puzzled her more than her position. She looked at the darkness, from where the voice came and said "I am a nurse here in the hospital. I came out to get some fresh air and while sneaking in maybe I got into a wrong tent. Who are you all? Why are you sitting in the dark? And what is that property of yours, which I might steal away?"

Her boldness of answering had some effect. The hands on her loosened. One strong voice said, "If you are a nurse what are you doing here? We know that, no one is allowed to go out. So tell the truth. What are you doing here, prowling like this in the night?"

This voice sent a sudden ripple of memory waves in her brain, down the memory lane and hit the target of recognition. In a rather delighted voice, she turned to the voice and said "Sir, Is that you? Are you Dr. Bhaskar Raju, the dean of DNA lab in Bangalore?" Now there was a hushed, surprised, quick breathing, in all of them.

The voice said "How do you know me? How can you identify me so well from my voice?" Ammu now got up and sat. One of them had switched on his wrist watch light and had half covered it so that they could see each other faintly. Ammu now saw eleven people mostly young seated on the ground in a circle, squatting, as if they were sitting for meditation. She looked straight at the eyes of Dr. Bhaskar Raju and said, "Sir, I know you very well because, last year, when you received the prestigious Raman award for your outstanding contribution to DNA research, from the President of India, I was your security, and stood near you for five hours."

Everyone was shocked as much as Dr. Raju. He said "Does it mean, you are not a nurse but….." Ammu completed the sentence for him. She said "Yes Sir. I am an officer from the crime branch and had entered here under the name of a nurse Ammu".

As everyone started talking, Dr Raju cautioned them and said "Please be quite for one second. Dr. Krishna, go and switch on music in your room" He got up fast and running to his cubicle put on the dim light and started his music system and came back.

Dr Raju said, "We are constantly watched during the day. So every night, we put off the light and hold a meeting here. We discuss our research, and also the possibility of a way of our escape" Then he told in short, their story, how they were deceived and abducted. The young doctor's eyes were now looking at her with anticipation and expectation of a solution.

Ammu said "Sir, if you people are given computers, why you did not try sending a SOS message to someone?" Dr Raju said "Ammu, these criminals are sharp. They had jammed all the signals going out from this area. Hence we can only receive data, but cannot send any signal outside. So there is no hope" Ammu looked at her wrist. She thought "That means Jadav sir would not have got any signal from my tracer. The tracer is of no use"

Dr. Raju added "These people use their own cell phone. They might have a separate signal source for that." Ammu looked at her watch. It was 4.30 in the morning. She said with urgency" Ok, I have to go now. I would try to come again. Mean while, you doctors accumulate as much chemicals as possible, the one which is inflammable, and the ones which can be used for attacks" She got up and walked back to the door as the doctors looked on.

Chapter 33

The Night adventure

Reaching the door, Ammu again went down on her stomach, and crawled out. She was now in two minds. Either she can go back to her bed, or she can go outside, make a little more survey. She had one clear hour in hand. She remembered what Dr Raju said. Every solder had a cell phone, and their signals could go out. That means, she had to get a cell phone, at any cost, from one of the solders. But how could she manage to do it? She started crawling again along the edge, of the tent towards the outside. She crawled, nearly for ten minutes, still did not see any guard. It might be possible, that being here for quite some time, the nurses and the patients know that there is no way to escape. Thus they had given up all hope, and decided, to go with their fate. Thus the criminals might have lessened their petrol duty. Still something was amiss. She stopped crawling, and rested for few seconds putting her head flat, on the ground. As her eyes were on level with the ground, something gleaming, in the mild moon light, got her attention. She inched slowly towards that. Just three steps away from the shining point she recognised it. She gasped. It was a land mine. Usually the land mines are buried deeply in the ground to hide them. But here, they did not bother to do that. The land mine was just there with a very small portion of it buried. A large portion was outside. So by chance, if anyone tries to escape, in the night, while running, they would definitely, step on one of them. With her eyes on level to the ground, she could see dozens of them, laid all over the length of the tent, very close to the wall. It would serve as a defense, if a rescue team lands up. She just remained there, flat on the ground thinking seriously. She heard a faint sound. Lifting her head, she saw two guards walking on opposite direction, from one.. They had their machine gun, slung across their shoulder, their fingers on the trigger, ready to shoot, as they lazily walked. The guards were walking at the base of the valley, nearly forty meters away from the tent.

Back in her police station days when she had her tight work schedule, day and night, she had a unusual strange fascination for which even Jadav always use to tease her. Given any opportunity even if she gets five minutes free, she would prefer to watch thriller movies in her PC or in her cell phone. Mostly she would watch just the climax scene if she don't have time for the full movie. She had seen that even the most stupid or impossible movies, sometimes gives out an excellent idea. She decided to use one of that ideas now.

She got up and started walking, making enough noise by stamping her feet hard. She walked dead straight, towards one of the guards. Only after five minutes, the guard noticed her. He was shocked for one moment, then he shouted, "Hey, you lady there, stop, I say stop just now!" But she walked on totally deaf to his shouting. Now in a irritated voice, he yelled louder, "Hey, lady, can't you hear me? Where are you going? Stop just now or I will shoot ". He lowered his gun, from the shoulder, to the shooting position. She still walked, her eyes wide open, her hand stretched outside like a blind person and she nearly reached him. The other soldier now heard the shouting and came running towards them. She walked close to him, seeing through him, and crossed over. Then suddenly she fell flat on her face, curled up, and stared snoring. The stunned guards, came near her, and looked down, unable to believe their eyes. The first guard said "Imagine! She is not even afraid of my shooting. She just walked on and on. Then now what is this? Why is she on the ground?" The second guard bend down, leaned close to her face, and examined her breathing and snoring. He said "This one seems, to be in deep sleep. She is snoring. May be she was sleep walking" "What will we do now?" the first one asked,

"Shall we try to wake her up?" The second one said "It is very difficult, to wake a person who is sleep walking. She seems to be a new nurse. Just carry her in, and put her in her bed. I will watch the place, till you come back"

The hefty guard lifted her, cursing her under his breath, and started walking towards the tent. He threw her roughly over his shoulder and carried her, as if, he was carrying a dead deer. Her both hands were dangling on his back loosely. She opened her eyes and carefully stretched her hand, to his hip pocket of the pants, and pulled out his cell phone. She slipped the phone inside her shirt and continued to pretend sleeping. The guard brought her inside and dropped her on the first empty cot. Having done that, he looked at her for one moment. Even in the dim light her milky skin, and chiselled innocent face, quickened his breath, and his pulse raced. But then the strict code of conduct they were to follow and the punishment if they failed made him turn and walk out.

Ammu waited for two minutes after the guard left. She got up, and started pulling her blanket over her head. She looked at the baby nurse. She was still awake, and she smiled. Going under the blanket, she took the cell phone and searched for the message menu. Then she started messaging in rapid jet speed.

> *"Fifty eight pregnant girls, sixty two nurses, seventeen doctors are captive in some unknown deep valley. No signal zone. Camp is wired with land mine. Criminals are in military uniform. Urgent, help needed. Entry to camp is some unknown secret passage"* **Sherya.**

She sent the message to Jadav's cell phone. The message took quite some time, to move and remained as it is. Her heart raced madly, and her breath quickened and her mouth went dry. She prayed hard with all her heart. Finally slowly the message went. She quickly went back to the menu and deleted the message. Then she held her breath and came out of the blanket. Once again she went down and rolled on the ground. Making quick rolling motion, she reached the door. She placed the cell phone, on the carpet, just next to the door and rolled back all the way. She reached her bed, climbed over and covered herself. Her heart was racing madly still. She fell asleep soon.

After five minutes the guard found that his cell phone was missing. He called his friend and told him. The other guard said "You could have dropped it when you carried that lady. Go and check. I will keep the watch" The guard came back looking all over the ground. When he just entered the tent, he noticed the cell phone on the ground. He picked it up and checked. Satisfied that it was not used, he returned to his post outside.

Chapter 34

Where are the missing scientists?

A heavily bleeding Ankita was rushed into the operation theatre, with serious head injuries. Her parents Madav rao and Ganga waited anxiously at the reception area. After half an hour, the doctor came out of the causality room. Madav Rao rushed to him and asked "Doctor how is Ankita? She is my daughter"

The doctor looked at his worried face, and then at the crestfallen Mrs. Rao, and said soothingly "Mr.. Rao, the situation is very critical. One good thing is that, you had brought her immediately, to the hospital, after the accident, and thus had prevented major blood loss. We have to operate her immediately. After her surgery we have wait, and watch, and her condition depends, on her body's response to the treatment. After the surgery we have to wait for minimum 48 hours to say anything. Where is her husband? We would need his signature on the consent form before surgery?"

Mr. Rao swallowed his tears and said "Sir, her husband Dr. Krishna is a scientist in the DNA institute and at the moment, out of station for some special project work. I would sign all the needed forms"

Doctor said, "That is fine, Mr. Rao. But inform him immediately, about the accident, as I told you, her condition is really critical" As he was talking, is eyes fell on the entrance and he said "Thank God, the neurosurgeon has arrived. Sir, you please finish the formalities, the nurse would help you."

He walked with quicksteps, towards the Neurosurgeon, and shaking hands with him, said "I am very happy doctor, that you could make it so fast. The patient is really critical." As they both walked past the reception, the Neurosurgeons saw Rao, and stopped. He said "Mr. Rao, what are you doing here? Strange meeting you here in hospital. Who is sick?"

Mr. Rao's face lit up, as he extended a hand, towards the surgeon. "Hello. Doc really strange, sorry, situation to meet" As they quickly exchanged the news of accident, Surgeon Menon patted the back of Rao affectionately, and said,

"Don't you worry Rao!. Nothing will happen to your daughter. Call your son in law Dr. Krishna as soon as possible" He walked briskly towards the operation theatre.

The operation dragged on for four hours. Rao and Ganga waited without sleeping all through the night. Early morning doctor came with a bright smile and said "Mr. Rao, good news. Ankita has come back to consciousness and is out of danger now. You can see her for just two minutes" They rushed into the room. Ankita, her head full in bandage, smiled at them. Next day the hospital vigil was taken over, by his second daughter. Dr Rao came home with Ganga. He told her "It is very strange Ganga! Krishna had gone for a project, which should have completed, by two months. Now ten months are over, and still there is no message from him. I can understand research information, could be classified. But why Krishna did not make a single phone call to Ankita? She never told us a single word about this. Luckily, Veena came to see her sister, and she was near her, at the time of accident. I am going to Krishna's office and find out about the project. We have to inform Krishna about the accident". Next day morning Rao visited the Rammayya DNA research institute. He met Mr. Prasad, the Admin head and said that he wanted to see the director Dr Bhaskar Raju.

Mr. Prasad looked surprised as he said, "Mr. Rao, didn't Mr. Krishna tell you about the project? The entire DNA office, all the eleven doctors, had gone for a research project nine months ago. Since the project was classified, they did not leave any address or telephone number" Mr. Rao sat still for some time. Then he asked, "Is anyone here, know something about the project?" Prasad called three of the assistants and every one replied in negative.

The lab assistant, watching all this came forward, and said "Sir, three days before all the doctors left, one senior military officer had come to meet our Sir" Rao was about to question while Mr. Prasad burst out "Oh God. I forgot to mention. One Mr. Tippu Chinnaiya, the director of the special research branch, Army, visited our office and had a long conversation with Mr. Raju".

Mr. Rao frowned as he asked "Research unit of Army? And they approached this institute? All works including, research and development, of Army are handled by only the Army doctors and officers. No job is handed to any civilian so far. This is strange." He thanked Mr. Prasad and walked away. Since the project was said to be connected to Militar, Mr. Rao, a retired colonel, thought he can get information directly from the military people. He straight away visited, the Army unit stationed in Bangalore. Using his identity, as a retired colonel, he asked for a permission, to meet Major general Karan Singh, with whom he had worked earlier. Karan sing welcomed him warmly. As Rao unfolded, the news of his son in law Dr. Krishnan, and his entire office of eleven scientists, vanishing for some strange project, General's eye widened in shock.

He said "Colonel Rao, I am afraid there is some grave mistake, somewhere. It is true that the Army was planning, to open a new research wing and Major General Rangappa, and not Tippu Chinnaiya, was going to be the director for that. This research project was meant for research in the invention of new war weapons and new modes of surveillance etc. No DNA research was ever mentioned, or planned. Anyway till now this project is still in the discussion stage only! So no doctors were employed, by the army, for any research. And I had never heard of this name Tippu Chinnaiya." Rao sat, very still, unable to digest the news. What will he answer to his daughter? Where is her husband? Major general Karan Sing said with sympathy "Colonel Rao, don't worry. I will get in touch with our vigilant department in Delhi today itself, and request to start investigating immediately. Not just Krishna but the entire DNA Institute doctors are involved and it is very serious. But rest assured, we would find out everything soon, and Krishna will return home safe." Colonel Rao could not believe it. Criminals, using the name of Indian Army, is the last thing anyone would dream of! He thanked the General and left with a heavy heart.

Chapter 35

The search for the camp

Jadav was flabbergasted, stunned beyond words to see the text message of Sherya. On one hand, there was immense happiness that she was alive still. On the other hand, the contents of the message were too much to digest, much less act on. He read it repeatedly, to make sure what he was reading was even possible. They knew that women were abducted in different places. However, here they were all pregnant! How did they manage to abduct so many pregnant women? And for what purpose? Then the doctors, nurses in all totaled about 140 people captive! He decided to call Commissioner Gadre to updates him on the latest development. At the same time, his cell phone started ringing, and surprisingly it was Gadre.

He said "I am taking an early morning flight tomorrow, and coming to your base. Something serious had turned up" He closed the line, without waiting, for any reply. Jadav could sense, the concern, anxiety and agony in Gadre's voice, "Oh God!" he said to himself. We are already up to neck in the mess, and now what is this new threat he had just now heard made him so worried. He had no alternative but to wait till next day morning.

The meeting of the special team of crime branch started early next day. Gadre drove straight from the airport to the venue. As the meeting began, Jadav informed the members about the message he had received from Sherya. The response was mixed, exactly, just like that of Jadav's. Happy because she is alive, and could manage to send a message, and shocked, because of the contents of the message. Rohit got up and said "Sir, 58 pregnant ladies? Horrible! How cruel of them, to abduct pregnant helpless, women?"

Milind said "Sir, what would be their motive, in capturing the pregnant women. This is most ridiculous kidnapping we had ever heard of?"

Gadre seemed particularly stressed, as he asked, "Jadav, has she mentioned anything about the place where they are captive?" Jadav said "Sir, yesterday when I got the message the night itself, I contacted the service provider of the cell phone and located the origin of the message. It is exactly the same spot, which I was zeroing on, or speculating. The spot is between the two tall mountains, the valley where we spotted one single light on our survey"

Gadre said "Assuming that camp is in valley, the question is how do we enter the den? We know that, there is no way of entering the camp, at least till now. If we drop the black cats from the helicopters, they would shoot us down before we reach the ground. You cannot climb down the mountain using experts because they would again spot us before we land. The only possibility is we should try attacking in the night. Is it even possible to scale the steep mountain down in the night, quietly and not be spotted"

Rohit asked "Sir, assuming that we go down, and over power the criminals, how would we rescue and transport so many, that too these pregnant ladies?" Jadav said, "There must be a secret passage somewhere through which, the criminals are going in and out. We have to find it out, and enter through the same way, and attack and rescue."

Gadre said "We had already combed the side of the mountain inch by inch. How do you propose to search now?" As everyone remained silent he continued "Well, I have some more shocking news to give" As every one's eyes turned towards him he said "I had got intimation from Delhi secret service that a group of eleven high level scientists from the Bangalore research centre are missing for the past eight months. They have vanished without any trace and even their families have no clue where they are" Dead silence prevailed.

Jadav said "Sir, I think they are also in this camp. That is what Sherya mentioned as eighteen doctors. It should be eleven of these plus other seven doctors" Every one sat tongue-tied.

Jadav said again "Sir, let us request the help of skilled black cats from Army or police. We would need a lot of ammunitions, laser guns with silencer, and other latest weapons. We would also place request for heavy army tanks, which withstand bullets. By the time we collect our material, and men I feel, Sherya may manage to send us another message" Gadre agreed. They started discussing and listing out for the needed force, men and materials.

Chapter 36

The hacking

Shankara Narayanan, the Director and head of the Tourism and Foreign Affairs secretariat, was one of the most respected IFS officers. He had a record of a long spotless service, and had served under various ministries and Governments, and all of them appreciated him. But today happened to be, an unprecedented day for him. Mrs. Gupta, his PA, was sitting across his table and both of them were, in the midst of a serious discussion. His phone, which was a unlisted, direct line from minister, jingled. It was the Minister for Foreign affair on the line. He said briefly "Shankar come to my room immediately" and closed the line even before he said "yes." Shankar got up straightened his tie and picking up his coat from the back of his chair, and wearing it, said

"Mrs Gupta, Minister has called me. We will continue the discussion after I come back" He once again checked his dress and opening the door, walked through the long corridor, very briskly towards the Minister's cabin. The security at the door of the Minister's cabin opened the door, and he walked in. As he entered, the minister looked up at him and said "Come in Shankar, take your seat." While entering its self, Shankar noticed, that there was another person, a foreigners, sitting in a chair on the side of the minister. As he sat, the minister said

"Shankar meet, Dr Martin from USA" and turning to Martin he said "This is Mr. Shankar, one of our best person" Both of them shook hands, and seated themselves. The minister started in a voice full of concern and worry

"Dr Martin is from the intelligence department of Washington. On their routine work of checking of signals from the group of the terrorist origin areas that of Taliban, Islamic revolutionary group, ISI, and many nameless cells, they happened to interpret signals, from India. The entire text of the code of the message could not be cracked, but it is understood, that a large group of terrorists, have set up a camp in India, and are planning something in a massive scale. They root their call signals crossing through many countries like Arabia, Pakistan, Iraq and other Islamic state, and hence it is difficult to trace, the exact location of their origin. They had managed to set up the camp, by entering our country, with tourist visa or Visa for attending conference or Visa for some medical treatment in Kerala. They have hacked our master computers, and forged Visa, and passport. The passports issued are all that of the listed dead persons." He stopped. Shankar was visibly shocked, and beads of sweat, appeared on his forehead, in spite of the high AC of the room. He murmured

"Sir, if such profound level hacking is done, there must be many persons from our department involved in this! How do we track them?" The minister said "That is why Martin is here. When our PM was informed by US, he had requested US for help, and they had sent Mr. Martin. He is the dean of the department in US, where they actually teach the Army to hack, for tracking down the potential hackers. He will be here in your office, working undercover, as an assistant to you, but in reality, he would go into our system, and track down the origin of hacking. Of course, it goes without saying, that this entire operation, is highly confidential, and will be known only to three of us"

Shankar had previously worked with lot of issues like scams, money laundering, telephone tapping of the ministers etc, but this one, was too hard, to swallow. His legs were a little unstable, when he walked back to his cabin with Dr. Martin. He called Mrs Gupta and said "Mrs Gupta set up a new cabin immediately. This is Dr Martin, from USA. He is a system analyst, and would be working, with us for some time. Give him all the needed things ----man power, computers, phone lines, cell phone —everything he wants for his work. He is our "A" listed officer. Please take very good care of him".

Dr Martin, thanked Shankar, and left with Mrs Gupta. After they left, for a long time, he continued to sit very still, unable to concentrate on any work, blankly looking at the walls, worried stiff.

Chapter 37

A friend in need

Ammu tirelessly continued her effort to make friendship with the patients. There was a very young girl, hardly fifteen, pregnant with triplets. She was not able to cope up with the changes in her body due to the development of the babies and one day when Ammu was helping her with bathing, she burst out crying. Ammu carefully kept the shower running, to muffle her voice and talked tenderly, all honey and sugar to the girl "Maya, please don't cry. Let me know where it is paining badly, and I would massage that part, and your pain will come down." She then gently massaged the stomach of the young girl, where the she was getting the cramps. The massaging under hot water, eased the pain, and Maya looked up at her face with gratitude and said "Thank you Ammu, the pain is better now" Ammu continued to massage and asked tenderly "Maya, Your age is for going to school and study. Why did you marry so early and get pregnant?" Maya looked up at her face, as if a scapegoat and fresh tears welled in her eyes, as she murmured, "I am not married sister." Ammu did her best to hide her shock and continuing the massage asked her "Then how did you get pregnant? You went out with some boy, who cheated and did this to you?"

Maya shook her head vigorously and said "No, Ammu, when I came here to this hospital I was not pregnant. I do not know, even now, how I got pregnant! After we came here they took some we girls for some medical test. And they told us that we are pregnant. Oh, my body is paining a lot. I think I am going to die soon" She burst out crying sobbing uncontrollably. Ammu, hugged her tight and consoled her "It is OK, Maya now it would be just one more month and then the babies would be born and you won't have any more pain" She patted Maya dry with a very gentle and caring hand and helped her to put on her dress. Seating her in the wheel chair, she wheeled her back to her bed. She went out for her tea break. When she came back from tea break the tea which Sona was giving her now without the drug she was in for a huge surprise. For the first time since her coming to the hospital both the patients, young girls, of her cubicle, gave her a broad smile. Maya said, "I am feeling much better now and this girl is Chinna" Ammu, was delighted beyond words, at the new friendship she had earned!

In the evening, one of the senior doctors, who had snapped her earlier, gave a warm smile and gave her a prescription while leaving. On opening the prescription, she saw the note, which read "Gokul told us everything. All we six doctors will cooperate with you. Count on us for any help" Ammu quietly destroyed the note. Next day, in a new cubicle, she helped the patient with tender massaging and talking and it broke the ice. She learnt that all the girls had become pregnant only after coming to the hospital. As she went around attending to her various normal duties, her head was restlessly bursting with two questions. Why are they made pregnant and how was that done without the knowledge of the girls? The girls did not say that they were raped! All the doctors knew now that all the solders around them are military uniformed disguised terrorists. What could be the motive of these terrorists, to go for such an elaborate plan to set up a whole hospital with nurses and doctors and take care of a set of the pregnant ladies? There was absolutely no answer! She looked at the chart on the bed of the patient and saw that for both the girls, delivery was due by one month. Next day she went to another cubicle, and found that their due dates were also the same. With hysterical, wild, inquisitiveness, somehow she managed to enter other cubicles one by one on some pretext or other, to read the charts and to her horror, found that all of those were due on the same month, on the same week. Fifty-eight young girls pregnant without their knowledge with twins or triplets, and were all due for delivery at the end of the present month, March!

She now realized that in spite of the complication and danger in the rescue, it had to be done at the earliest, before these girls deliver. Once they delivered, then with so many tiny babies, the rescue mission would be next to impossible. As if an answer to her prayer, Gokul arrived at her cubicle.

He said curtly "Ammu, just hold the hands of this patient, tightly. She is not allowing, me to take the pressure." Ammu went down on her knees, her shoulder brushing against Gokul's and held the girls hand pressed on the cot. Gokul leaned towards her his face so close, that she could feel his breath and softly whispered, "I got a plan, somehow you have to get four or five patients on our side who would be ready to do whatever we ask them"

Ammu murmured, "I got six girls' Gokul started removing, the blood pressure monitor and murmured "These girls are victims like us. But don't trust the nurses. Some of them may be the camp people" He finished his examination, and went away. In the tea break, as she walked towards the reception she found Gokul coming in front of her from the opposite direction. He seemed totally indifferent to her presence looking away in some other direction and crossed her and walked away. But when he crossed her he brushed against her, and stuffed a tiny note in her hand. She squeezed and rolled the given note from the grip of her palm to the tip of her fingers and pretending to straighten her shirt button, slipped the paper carefully into her shirt. Going back to the Cubicle, she sat back on her chair and waited patiently. Once the patients started sleeping, she pulled the note and read it. She read it again and again three times to make sure of what is needed. Then she destroyed the note.

Next day helping Maya and Chinna in the bath she whispered the needed message. She volunteered to help bathing of two more girls whom she had befriended and repeated the same message. As she wheeled their wheel chairs to their Cubicle, Gokul again appeared in front of her. She looked at him for a second then talked to Maya "Everything is fine Maya don't worry" Gokul walked away. Ammu looked at her watch. There was one hour for lunch. And, one hour, for their first step of operation to begin!

Chapter 38

Visitor from Nepal

It was just the second week of March, and Delhi was reeling, under unbearable heat wave already. It was after noon, and the streets were nearly deserted, as people preferred to stay in door. But the in the tiny butcher shop, the business was as usual. The hard working Gaffer Baba, was working as usual. A mini old fan on the ceiling of the tiny shop, made more noise than breeze. An auto came and stopped in front of the shop. Khan got out with a Nepali youth. Baba stopped his chopping and silently watched them. Both of them climbed the shop steps. Baba walked to the bench on the backside and sat. He signaled to the Nepali to come to him. Khan stood at the entrance watching the street up and down.

Baba asked "How many this time?" Nepali opened the bundle he was carrying. He said "Baba I could manage only 68. Here are their identity cards, either ration card or work ID card, or bank card. I have taken all their finger prints in separate sheets and labelled them" As Baba nodded, he tied back the bundle again.

Baba asked in a deep voice "The news was that hundreds of people in Nepal died in the earth quake. Then why is that you could manage, only this much?" The Nepali looked around nervously and whispered "Baba, people were flocking around every dead person like hawks, for getting the compensation. With great caution, we could capture some relatives and got these records. Our men are still there on the spot, trying. As I got your urgent message I came with the things I had already collected so far" Baba grunted. He looked at Khan, and said "Take him home pay, and send him off. Make arrangement, for this bundle to be despatched, to our party". When both of them left, he returned to his relentless, chopping, as if whatever happened was nothing important.

Chapter 39

Panic hits the hospital

The lunch was served in the hospital at 1.30 PM sharp every day. Post lunch, Ammu pretended to be busy tried very hard to suppress the desire to look at the watch again. Time ticked on and reached 2.15 pm. An ear-piercing scream erupted from Maya's cubicle. Ammu and two sisters rushed to the cubicle. They found that Maya was going into violent convulsions. The red button was pressed and a doctor rushed in to examine her. Instantly there was another scream from one more patient and then a third one and a fourth one. Doctors rushed madly from patient to patient to attend. Injections were given and the oxygen masks were pulled over the faces to control the convulsion. Five patients falling sick, violently, at the same time! The hospital was shaken up!

Four uniformed nurses, all the seven doctors, and nearly all the nurses skirted around the affected patients. Half a dozen solders with rifles also rushed in. The uniformed sisters looked at the seven doctors and shouted "What is happening doctor? Why did they become sick? You know how important they are for us!. Have you not given them proper medication? Answer fast"

The doctors were engaged in a group discussion among themselves, and impatiently said "Please keep quiet for some time. We are trying to find the reason"

The way they snapped back, shocked the uniformed nurse. They waited. After five minutes of discussion Dr Gokul came forward and said "Sister! We have a very bad news to give you. These girls have contacted a serious viral infection. This is very contagious and after some time all the patients might contact this"

The sister screamed and yelled their vocal chords bursting. "How could this happen? How?? We are maintaining, the most sterile environment. Then how could this happen? I don't know what you would do! Just now stop the spreading of the virus and save the ones who are affected."

Gokul said calmly with a deep concern in his voice "Sister, these viral attacks can happen anywhere for any one. These girls are pregnant and have low immunity!. It may be shocking. But the reality is if not treated immediately and properly by twenty four hours all of them would die!"

The sister now banged her head with her hands and said "Treat doctor, treat them immediately. What are you people waiting for?"

Another doctor now said "But Sister, where is the medicine for treating? We had just given the available Injection for the time being. But…"

Gokul took over and said "None of us anticipated or expected this viral attack. Hence we had not stocked the needed large quantity, of antibiotic injection. We may need more than a thousand injections. Because now, each and every patient, had to be injected, every two hours, for five days, consecutively! Otherwise we have to just stand and watch them dying"

The three uniformed nurses pooled together and discussed. Then she said again" You doctors make a list of the needed medicine right away. Our men would go and get it immediately"

Just then, there was one more scream, and one after other, two more patients fell sick. The uniformed nurse took her cell phone and made a hushed, conversation. From her face Ammu could make out that the person on the other end of the line was screaming, at the top of his voice, firing her left, right and centre. She politely begged, repeatedly and closed the line.

Gokul waiting for the conversation to end now said "Sister this much of medicines would not be available from any shop immediately. You have to place an order and wait for two days. But by then it would be too late and we may lose more than half of our patient"

After getting a firing from her boss the uniformed nurse was highly nervous, anxious and her voice was worried and strained as she said "Then please tell me doctor what is the option left for us?"

Gokul said "Ok there is one solution. Two of us we doctors, would go personally and pick up the medicine for this immediate emergency. Same time, we would place order for more of medicines for future use"

Nurse said "But why should you doctors, had to go for that"

Gokul said "As I told you we need injections immediately, minimum 1000 numbers!. You know, that a specific medicine could come with various combinations and dosage. In an emergency we can use any one medicine in place of other and get at least some benefit. Only we doctors can read the labels, and pick up the alternative medicines, from hundreds of combination. Neither can we list out a thousand combinations, nor your non- medical solders can pick them up, and you are going to lose patient every passing minute just because of your indifference"

He finished his talking, and shrugging his shoulders, showing utter indifference, turned to other doctors and said" Doctors, we are left with no option but to watch helplessly our patient die one by one. In this hospital, where, non medical people give orders we cannot do anything else" Saying this he started walking away.

The sister now came running behind him, and started pleading "Ok! OK" you doctors can go for buying the medicine, but only one of you can go!. The others are needed here for help"

Gokul said "In that case I would go for selecting the medicines as other doctors are seniors and more experienced. But at least send one nurse with me, who can select the medicine along with me"

As the uniformed sister, looked around Ammu came forward, and said "Madam, I would go with the doctor. In the Kerala hospital, where I was working earlier, the same viral infection attack happened. So I know three or four combinations of medicines that can be used" She kept her face very impassive, absolutely blank, when her heart was racing painfully, waiting for the positive answer.

Gokul said "Come on sister decide fast please, we are losing time"

At the same time Maya started screaming once again and doctors rushed to her. The sister said "OK, both of you go. But get the medicines as early as possible. Our solders would be coming with you. So don't try anything funny to annoy them"

Gokul and Ammu were escorted out and the tin door through which she had entered on her first day opened. They stepped out in the corridor. Six armed guards walked closely with them. They reached the main gate. An ambulance was waiting with its engine roaring ready to move. As they climbed inside the ambulance, shot out in full speed. Gokul and Ammu sat on two extreme ends, with all six solders, sitting between them. Both of them carefully, avoided their eye contact, and looked in different directions. Ammu thanked God, for the completion of the first part of their plan.

Chapter 40

The Final action

It was mid night, two thirty in the night. The young man's special unlisted, telephone jingled. He woke up from sleep and sat upright. His heart started pleading "Please, don't take the call. Ignore it. Pretend to be sleeping" But he knew that he couldn't do that. He reluctantly walked, to the phone and as he picked up, the voice from other end, started without waiting for his hello. The voice was very deep and whispering. But he felt that it was like a icy razor cutting through him.

The voice said "Beta, what is this I am hearing? You said that you wanted time? You know that for my job, there is no waiting time. Are you becoming crazy or something?" The young man swallowed hard and murmured "But Baba, everything, is not in my hand. I had to depend on my log head. He is routing it through at least thirty points to get the need finalized. He told me that the 68 number is very high for a dead line of one week. And ….."

Baba cut him short. "Beta, I don't want to go in to the details. We are not government bodies who had to take a lot of time to process. If log head is not efficient, knock him off and hire someone new. There are many hungry people out there waiting for a job and with the finance we are providing it should be kid's job….." A hacking cough interrupted his talking and he stopped talking. The young man said with concern "Baba, why don't you take some treatment, and some rest. Your health is turning bad, day by day"

Baba retorted angrily, "Stop worrying about me! My mission is my life, and before my last breath, I should complete it"

The young man spoke again "Baba, the problem is that, you have got all Nepalese persons id cards this time! These men look distinctly different, and our men will not fit in that slot. Remember Thippu, how hard it was to forge his name!"

Baba snapped back "It is your job to worry. Before I forget, remember the Visa's had to be split like last time in different groups --tourist, for attending conference or for participation in cultural activities. OK, God bless you my son" The phone went dead.

The young man now dialled an unlisted number and had a long conversation, filled with arguments, pleading, threat etc. It was five 'O' clock in the morning, as he finished. He decided not to go back to bed. He walked to the Jesus Christ photo hung on the wall and knelt down. As he prayed, tears rolled down from his eyes. He got up and opened his table drawer. There was a partly blackened photo in a frame. He looked at the half burnt picture!. The entire past scene again flashed in his mind. He wished that he had burnt to ashes in the fire along with his parents.

Chapter 41

The medical shop

As the ambulance moved fast, for the first time Ammu could see the path of their travel. Coming out of the long corridor, the ambulance entered a narrow cave, which was lighted all the way. When they reached the dead end of the cave, the driver took up his cell phone and said a single word "Open" Ammu's heart jumped out of her chest cavity, at what she saw. A rounded tin door slid open, and revealed a path just enough for the ambulance to go out. The moment they were out of the gate, the driver again called on his cell phone and the tin gate silently slid back. Ammu just stared, unable to digest what she saw. The tin door from the outside was pasted with pieces of rocks, real or may be artificial one, all over. At the bottom of the tin door, there was some hidden grill on which a number of short shrubs and creepers were planted. The grill was heavily covered with creepers. The camouflage was so good that from outside they could see only the solid mountain rock with no trace of any cave. The ambulance started climbing down the hill through the rough terrain. She though "This is the secret passage through which only the terrorist could enter. And the valley is unreachable by anyone else." They now moved, through small villages and finally the ambulance stopped. It had taken one and half hour for them to reach this point. The solders got out and Gokul and Ammu followed the suit.

It was a newly opened medical shop at the outskirts of the town. A nursing home was under construction just nearby. Hence this new shop was made a bit larger than the usual ones with two large rooms. The shop keeper looked up and was shocked as half a dozen, gun bearing military solders, entered the shop suddenly.

One of them approached the shop keeper and said "We have come from a nearby military rifle range shooting practise camp. There is an emergency and some our soldiers had fallen sick. Our doctor has come with us to pick up the medicine. Give them whatever they wanted and don't worry about the price" He gestured to Gokul and Ammu to come inside. He looked at Gokul and ordered "Doctor, Pick up medicines as fast as you can. For the balance of the, remaining drugs place an order"

The shop keeper said politely to the solder "Sir, when the doctors pick up the medicine would you mind waiting outside? My other customers might get disturbed by your solders and your gun" The solder grunted and said "OK doctor, we would wait in the van."

Five of them climbed back into the van and only one remained inside the shop, keeping his gun hidden under his legs. Gokul startled asking for the name of so many injections, so rapidly, that the two shop keepers, found it difficult, to attend on him. The counter was piled with boxes and Gokul was carefully reading and checking into the combination of every boxes. He looked up at the shopkeeper and asked "Do you have more stocks in the next room?. My nurse would pick them up, straight from the boxes, so that we can finish faster".

The shopkeeper nodded and said "Yes Doctor, It is a good idea! Madam, you please come with me to the next room. Some of the parcels are yet to be opened. You can pick up the boxes directly" Ammu, walked with him to the next room.

The solder got up, and followed them to the next room. Ammu started putting her head into the large carton boxes, sticking her head deep, and asking the assistant, what she wanted. The solder watched for some time felt satisfied and walked back to his bench in the first room.

Along with Ammu, the assistant's head was also closely buried inside the carton box, just next to her, as he tried to help her. She looked up, pointed to a corner box and said, "See that box, on the corner, I think that is the what, we are looking for"

She now moved, to the extreme corner, in the interior of the room. As the assistant opened the box she brushed close to him with both their heads inside the tall carton box, she whispered softly "Listen Brother, listen to me carefully, without showing any reaction" The shop keeper looked, at her for one second, and again burying his head inside, said "Yes Madam tell me". Ammu whispered back, "The soldiers sitting in military uniforms outside there are not real military persons. They are hard core criminals disguised in uniform and are now keeping number of people as captive."

The assistant gasped, and tried to talk something. Instantly, she cupped his mouth, with her hand and said "Don't talk, just listen. I am a police officer and just now I need your help now. Give me your cell phone"

Without a word he picked up his cell phone and handed it with a shivering hand. She said in a urgent voice "In case the soldier comes back here to check, give cover to me and keep pretending to be working."

When she entered this room itself she had noticed a wash room at the corner. Now she rushed inside and locked the door. Her heart was racing with joy, at the moment's success. She calmed herself and dialled Jadav's number. He picked up and seeing an unknown number answered in an indifferent voice "Hello, who is this?" For one second her heart melted, at the sound of that deep, familiar, voice. She controlled herself, and whispered "Sir, it's me." Jadav jumped out of his chair, too excited, and impatiently fired questions in a jet speed "Sherya, Sherya, Where are you,? How are you and ...."

She stopped him half way and urgently, and said

> *"Sir, please, please, only just listen! I don't have time. Tomorrow evening we would come to collect medicines to this same shop at the same time. You would need three large Army bullet proof vans, laser guns, hand grenades, and lots of ammunition, at least a battery of forty men from the SWAT and every one of you should be disguised in our Army uniforms for our rescue operation. Only by following, the terrorist's van you can enter the camp through the secret passage and......"*

Ammu urgently cut off her conversation and held her breath, as she heard the sound of heavy boots approaching. The solder came back to the second room to check on Ammu. Not finding her there he shouted at the shopkeeper whose head was still inside the box in a rude, rough voice "Hey you, Where is that girl?"

The shop keeper calmly raised his head from the box and with a most innocent face said "Sir, that Madam is seriously sick sir. She started throwing out. Just now only she went into the wash room"

Ammu was hearing every word spoken outside and now she opened the sink pipe to a maximum and made enough coughing and gurgling noise of coughing and throwing out. The solder banged the washroom door and said "Hey you lady, Come out immediately"

Jadav was hearing all this conversation happening from the other side of the line. Ammu put off the cell phone and slipped it into her shirt. Splashing water liberally all over her face she came out panting, looking very pale and sick and pretended as if she was about to collapse. The shop assistant rushed to her, and supporting her, said "Sister you please sit down. I will get some ice water for you",

For all this drama the solder stood there, stared at her and then grunting under his breath walked out. The assistant brought her a glass of water. As she took it, she murmured "Thank you so much" She looked around and making sure that the solder is out of sight, she gave the cell back and said "Once we had left, call the last number, I have called, and give this address, land mark to reach the place" She came to the front room of the shop, where Gokul was still searching.

The owner of the shop, looked at her and said "Madam I think it is better if I would load all the injections available with us. Otherwise, so much time would be wasted in searching, and you say that you have an emergency situation. Tomorrow we would get all the medicines in large quantity as you needed" The solder took out, a big wad of currency, and left it on the counter and said

"Bring these boxes of medicines to the van" He walked away to the van and three other shop boys started loading all parcels unopened, as it is, inside the van. The shop keeper came close to her, and whispered "Madam the moment they entered itself, I had my doubt. My father was in Army, and I know that Army would not buy medicines from outside shop, and would not have civilians as doctors, and would never carry Arms around" She looked at him and smiled. The soldiers were busy in loading. The assistant standing nearby said "I would do my best to help madam" Gokul was standing near the van, watching the loading. As Ammu joined him he looked at her face and said

"Ammu, you look very sick. Hope you have not contacted the viral infection from those patients!" Startled, she looked up and she noticed the mischief glint in his eyes. They all got into the van and the journey back to the camp started. The soldiers were really worried that she had contacted the virus and all of them sat together away from her. They pushed Ammu to the corner next to Gokul. As the van rushed on she moved close to him and her eyes still on guards she whispered

"Job is done". Gokul whispered "Thank God for his mercy"

Chapter 42

The preparation

Jadav sat frozen speechless after hearing Sherya's message. He had heard the shoulder's shouting voice and hoped and prayed that she was safe. Just after fifteen minutes the phone started ringing again and it was the same number. He took up the phone hesitantly and waited without answering. It is quite possible, that the terrorist had taken the phone, and is now checking up the number. But the voice calling said with urgency "Sir, I am the medical shop owner. Your madam called you some time back only from my shop"

Jadav, still answered non-committed "Oh, Is that true?"

The boy continued "Sir, madam asked me to call you and give the address of this shop. Sir, please note down. It is. ...." He gave the addresses of the shop and the land marks, roads to be taken, all in detail. Jadav asked him more questions about the terrorist, how they looked, how many were there, etc and boy answered in detail. Jadav thanked him, and told him to call his number again, if he observes anything suspicious, or if he is in danger, and closed the line.

Within half an hour, the special team sat for the meeting. Gadre was still there in the town, and thus became advantageous, for the team. Jadav started "From what Sherya said and the shop keeper reported, these terrorists are all disguised, as military persons. When they wear the Army uniform and move around with weapons, mostly the common man would never question them. This is the advantage they had used"

Gadre said "Now let us see what is going to be our plan and how do we attack them? We had earlier seen, that there is no way for attacking the valley without hurting the hostages"

Jadav answered "Sir, that is why they had played on, this medicine trick. They had promised to come for more medicines tomorrow. This is the chance opened for us. Tomorrow evening we have to wait in the medical shop, and ambush these men, when they come for the medicine. Then we had to stick

124

to them and go in their own vehicle, to enter the den. This is the only way the secret passage they are using would be accessible to us for entering. She had asked for specially three Army Large trucks, which should be also bullet proof. I think her idea is to make the captives nearly 200 in number to escape in these vans. It should be bullet proof because if the terrorist start firing at the van, the captives would not be injured"

Gadre said "I would immediately talk to the commissioner in Delhi, and see that we get all the needed uniforms, trucks, and ammunition. Our team has 18 members. We would request for one full regiment of the riot police unit, or if they agree, then the commandos to help us in this operation. Jadav I would leave now. You and the team plan the strategy of attack in detail".

The team sat together and drew different types of plan of attack, as the situation calls for. Jadav said "According to Sherya, the entire campus is wired. Hence right in the beginning, we have to attack the guards one by one, and over power them. The gun fire noise can alert the criminals and they may injure the victims, and start a war. Hence we would use only the physical attack or the silencer guns. Secondly, the gun fire could also start a major fire"

Murali said with appreciation, "Sherya, madam, had done such a great a great job, by taking a high risk, and reaching us this information"

Jadav said "Yes our officer is smart! But there must be some more persons, may be doctors, who had helped and created some situation, for the need of the medicine. The medical shop boy told me, that there was one doctor with her that day"

There was a call from Gadre. He said that he had got the clearance from Delhi, and all of them should immediately report to the military regiment. Within ten minutes, right at the dead of the night, they all moved to the nearby town. Time was a very important factor of any operation. Next day evening they had to start, the unheard great rescue operation, and as the first step, had to take their position, at the medical shop. The military officers were deeply involved as they know how it is to fight a war, and were ready to offer all the help needed. Besides the needed military uniforms, Jadav's group was also given, the latest laser silencer guns, laser goggles, hand grenade and guidance in using them effectively. Besides Jadav's twenty crime branch team, forty men from rapid action force joined them for the operation. A bomb diffusion team of fifteen too joined the group. They worked united with a fierce dedication. An anger smoldered in their hearts to burn every one of the terrorist alive.

Chapter 43

The hope

As the next day dawned the captives looked up at the sun with lots of hope, during their usual sun bath. Yesterday after coming back from the medical shop, all the seven doctors had started injecting the patients from the huge pack of medicines bought. Every pregnant lady was injected every three hours even when they did not show any symptom. This showed that they wanted to arrest the infection at any cost. The ones who had shown the infection symptom earlier also now calmed down. The fact that the injections were only water and were injected into the bed and not in the hands of the patient was known only to the patient, and the doctors. The possibility of escape kindled the die-hard fire in their belly and every nurse and patient co operated with a feverish pace. The fuming anger in their hearts of being victimized for such a long time now smoldered and gave them all an extra ounce of courage. Tiny notes of information written on match stick size paper passed on from hand to hand and everyone knew what they had to do and when to do. Gokul went to the adjoining tent, the one of the research doctor's tent, in the pretext of getting more sprit for injection, and the message was delivered to them too.

The military uniformed nurses waited for the evening when the rest of the medicines were suppose to arrive, hardly knowing that all the hostages were also restlessly waiting, for that special evening! Ammu, Baby nurse and Sona had carefully distributed the apt instruction to everyone.

For the patients the short note read "Get into a wheel chair the moment you hear the word "Fire", escape, and get into the van outside" For the nurses it read as" Help the patients to get on the wheel chair and pushing them run as fast you can, get into the van and never ever look back" For the research scholars, no specific instruction was given, but was told to attack and run, when they hear the word "Fire" The time ticked on.

The four military uniformed nurses were going round all the time checking the patients, and were relieved that the infection was quite under control. Taking advantage of their distraction, the nurses moved up down and a number of injection alcohol bottles were smuggled (A large number of them, were specially brought yesterday, with the medicine supply). The nurses smuggling the bottles quietly hid them under the bed sheet of the first cot meant for the night sister's rest. This chosen cot was the one, which was just next to door curtain, on the side of the hall. Besides this every nurse, managed to steal and hide one injection syringe filled with a heavy dose of sedative medicine in their pant pocket, as told. The whole air was charged with anticipation, apprehension and anxiety about the operation and as the time passed the waiting was becoming impossible. But in the deepest core of heart all of them had decided to fight even if means death. They now preferred to die fighting rather than live as a slave. Time ticked on and on.

Chapter 44

Mid night action

The minister for Foreign affairs and tourism was having hush- hush a serious meeting with his men in a closed room with Shankar and Dr. Martin. Besides Dr. Martin and Shankar there were three more trustworthy IAS officers in the meeting. Dr. Martin and his team had finally traced the origin, of the hacking point. They had identified 28 points at various levels, where the hacking was done, to change data, in the master computer, and feed illegal inputs. Besides the regular employed people there were 32 people who were outside the office engaged, in various normal occupations as an eyewash, but in reality, worked and completed the job for the terrorists. After discussion for some time the Minister said "Since this is the job of insiders even when we try to arrest or go for a raid, these people will get the wind and our operation might fail! So, immediate action is the only option. I had already requested the Inspector general of police over the line and he would be here at any moment" He hardly finished his sentence when there was a knock at the door and Inspector general Suvkvir Singh entered. Once he was seated, Dr Martin opened his list and systematically named all the persons involved, first the outsiders and then the persons employed with Ministry. He started from the lowest rung and finally disclosed the head of all operation the IAS officer. Except Dr. Martin, all others sitting the room were shocked to hear that name! Shankar said in a quivering voice "This boy? Surely is that this one, the young fellow? I had personally trained him when he joined service and had always admired his hard work and integrity. And he had done this?"

Mr. Singh also added "Yes sir, I had also interacted with him so many times in case of security of PM or other ministers etc. He was so well respected and was one of the best"

Minister said "Mr. Singh, I would request you to take action to night itself. It is 6.30 PM now. By three hours you pool all your resources, the best man of action in all the teams, and simultaneously raid all the 60 of these persons, one team for every individual person. That way any one of them would not have time to warn other. And as you know the matter has to be absolutely confidential, please" Some more details were discussed and the meeting ended.

The young man was just getting ready to wind up his office duty, when his unlisted cell buzzed softly. He looked at the watch, without picking up the call and murmured "Why this time and that too in the office!" He got up and locked the office cabin and then picked up the phone. He listened silently. The voice on the other end whispered one word. "The fire is lit" The phone went dead. He sat down heavily, seriously thinking for some time. Finally he murmured to himself "Thank you Jesus, that I planned everything the last week itself and thank you once again Jesus, that I could take a decision with courage"

He got into his car and called a number. He said "As I told you two day's back an urgent meeting is needed. Everyone is going to the get a huge amount of money as promised, today itself. Inform everyone to be present at ten thirty sharp, in the usual meeting place"

Then he drove calmly through the small gullies of Delhi. He parked his car at a distance far away from the Jugi and walked the remaining distance. He reached the Jugi and knocked. Khan opened the door and Baba sitting on the cot, looked up surprised. "Beta! What happened that you had come suddenly without intimation? You generally use to telephone and come."

He said "Sorry, Baba, some new customers had come. They want three pieces, immediately. Please ask Khan to get them for me just now itself".

Baba smiled "Beta, you are becoming smart now! Good, good" He turned to Khan and asked him to get what the young man asked. Khan got up and opening the door left the hut. The young man got up and closed the door. He then came close to Baba and said "Baba, for all the kindness you had done to me so for I am thankful to you and I can never ever repay back for them"

He knelt down at the feet of Baba and touched his feet. Baba was moved and he started "Beta, but this was only ...." But, before he could finish his sentence, the young man pulled the trigger of his silencer gun aiming right at his heart. Baba's eyes bulged out with surprise as his hand held the heart blood gushing all over his hand and stammered "Why you did this to me, why Beta?"

The young man said "I am very, very sorry Baba, But I am tired of cheating my country"

As Baba collapsed, he gently laid Baba's body on the cot closed his eyes. Covered him up with a sheet and touched his feet once again. He walked to a chair and waited. Khan entered after some time. Seeing Baba on the cot he said "Baba went to sleep so fast?" He walked towards the cot. The young man now shot Khan three times and he collapsed even without a moan. He wiped his gun calmly and came out. He closed the door tightly. He walked back, reached his car, and drove away. He reached home and had a good shower. Then he lighted two large candles in front of Jesus and knelt down with his head bend and remained in that position for a long time. He got up and walked to his table and sitting on his chair, wrote a long letter.

The time was 9.30 PM. He took two heavy bags and getting into the car, drove through the narrow by lanes of Delhi for twenty minutes. He parked his car in the shadow. Walking quite a distance, carrying the heavy bags, he reached an old, dilapidated, deserted, two story building. He climbed a flight of stairs to the first floor and knocked. The door opened. He saw that a large group of the members were already present there. He called the log head, and asked whether everyone had come because the money could not be distributed until everyone was present. The log head assured that all 57 members had come. He now kept the two heavy bags he was carrying, on the long table and said

"Thank you my friends for all the help you had done so for. I am very happy to distribute the money to all of you today". Looking at the log head again he said "Take this list. Call the names one by one and hand over the packet kept ready for them." He sat down and watched, as log head called the names one by one and from and paid them their cover. There was happiness all around. When the fourth name was called his cell phone started ringing. He picked it up and tried to listen saying "Hello, hello"

He looked at the log head and said "You continue to distribute the money. I am not getting signal for my cell phone. I would go out and take the call. All of you stay put till everyone gets their share. Then I would like to give all of you my special bonus from my own side".

He got up and went out of the room and stepped down the stairs, holding the cell still saying "Hello, hello" all the time. He had now come out of the building and making sure that no one was watching him, he quickly ran through the shadow about ten meters away from the building. He fished out a tiny remote from his pocket. Remote in hand he waited for a fraction of a second, took a deep breath and pressed it. Instantly there was a deafening explosion followed by a series of explosions. The old building, from which he had walked out a few minutes ago, was totally engulfed in raging fire. He stood there calmly for a few second, watching the fire. Having satisfied himself that no one came out or escaped from the building, he got into his car and rode away.

Right at the mid night the crime branch team went simultaneously for their raid to each and every house of the listed person. But they were in for surprise as they found none of the men in their house. The team which reached Gaffer's house, found both Gaffar and Khan shot dead.

Chapter 45

The first blow

At four thirty, the next day, the ambulance with Gokul and six solders, left for the medical shop, to collect the extra medicines for which orders were placed the previous day. The ambulance reached the medical shop without any event. They stopped in front of the medical shop and five of the solders sitting on the back side jumped out. Gokul got out leisurely and standing near the ambulance, cautiously, looked around. Yesterday when they came to the medical shop the area on the opposite side of the shop was a barren land of small stones and sand. But today, in that same space, there were five trees, and a thick cluster of heavy short bushes looking almost like a jungle, which all had appeared just over night.

When the solders reached the shop they found huge boxes packed up to the ceiling height. As they looked shocked the shop keeper said calmly "Sir, your doctors had ordered enormous amount of medicines. These are the medicines what your doctors had ordered." Three solders started lifting the boxes, and two went back and stood on the side of the ambulance talking to each other. Two pair of eyes from the bush were watching them and in a flash pulled the trigger of their silencer gun. Both the solders buckled and collapsed without even a moan. With lightening speed four pairs of hands crawled out of the bush and pulled the dead solder's bodies behind bush. At the same moment two uniformed soldiers from the hidden group crawled out and took the position of the dead near the ambulance. As Gokul watched all this he had to try very hard to control his racing heart. The three soldiers came back and started loading the box. Two swift bullets now fired from the inside of the boxes, knocked off two of them. Before the third one realised what was happening he too was shot dead by Jadav. All the three bodies were dragged, and loaded into a van hidden, behind the bushes by the solders of Jadav, who all had come out now. Two military bullet proof vans waiting at a distance moved in and joined the already parked van parked behind the ambulance. A lot of empty boxes were loaded into all three vans. Twenty solders jumped inside every van. Jadav now looked at Gokul standing near the ambulance. Gokul came forward and said "I am Dr. Gokul who ordered the medicines" That short sentence explained everything to Jadav.

He said "You give cover for me, and get into the front seat" The driver soldier sitting all this time in the driving seat was blissfully unaware of the things taking place in the back side. Jadav pulled his cap down on his forehead covering his half face. He climbed in to the front seat near the driver and sat very close to him. Gokul got in and slamming the ambulance door shut said "All medicines are loaded. We can go back now."

The driver not suspecting the new solder asked Gokul "Why two of you are coming to the front seat?"

Gokul said "There is so much medicine boxes to be carried that we have called for two more ambulances, and loaded all of them"

The solder looked out of the driver's window at the military vans and said in a confused voice "But I am not aware of the new vans! Let me get down and ask my other solders"

Before he made a move, Jadav pressed his gun on the driver's neck and ordered in a harsh voice "Just drive, if your life is precious for you! All your soldiers, are already gone to other world"

The solder was too scared, and was not prepared, for this sudden attack. He quietly started the ambulance and all Jadav's team, dressed in military uniform, hidden inside boxes in the three vans started moving. The three vans drove on, one behind the other and reached the cave mouth. As the solder started telephoning, Jadav pressed the gun harder and said "Be careful of what you talk. After asking for opening the gate, keep it as it is open"

The three vans entered one behind other through the gates and then the gate remained open still. Jadav looked at the spot where the cave started. He had a sinking feeling that he had his team had reached the same spot. They could not proceed ahead because of the camouflage of the plants kept over the tin door. The vans drove through the long cave. The rapid action police officers in all the three vans now became ready for attack with their laser guns ready to shoot.

Gokul said "Sir, would you please give me one gun?" As Jadav looked at him with a surprise he said "Sir, shooting is one of my hobbies. I am a state level champion"

Jadav took out a gun from the four guns he had thrust in his pocket and Gokul immediately hid it in his Doctor's coat pocket. As the first ambulance, neared the gate of the camp Gokul whispered "Sir we are reaching the gate. Force the driver to allow, all our three extra vans"

Jadav pressed the gun harder and hissed between his clenched teeth "Tell your gate security that three extra ambulance with medicines had come according to head quarter's order. If you try to signal or do something I will tear your head with my bare hand itself"

The driver was already half dead. A bunch of five soldiers came running near the ambulance and said "Hey, what are these extra vans for?" The driver said in a firm voice "Your doctors had ordered so much medicine that we have to call the head quarter and got these extra vans"

Gokul got down from the ambulance and said to the solders "Please unload the medicines fast! We need them urgently". Jadav stayed in the van. Terrorist solders in group of fours went to towards all three vans and moved to the back side for unloading. As one by one they tried to lift the box, they all fell down dead silently by the shots of the solders hiding inside. Jadav pulled the trigger on the driver, and got down from the van. He noticed that there were three terrorist solders near the gate. Their attention was on the backside of the three vans. Jadav knocked two of them in a quick succession. The third one noticed his friends collapsing and as he was about to raise an alarm, Gokul shot him, his gun still inside the coat. There were no more solders in sight. Gokul gestured Jadav with the nod of his head, the small room where the duty solders sat. Both of them walked in very calmly. Two uniformed ladies were sitting there. One looked up and said "Doctor has the medicines arrived?"

Gokul said "Yes Madam, they all have arrived" As he kept them engaged in his conversation Jadav standing behind him shot both of them in quick move. Now all the police force jumped out of the van and pooled in the gate area. Jadav gave quick instructions breathlessly.

He said "Three of you reverse the three vans, and park them facing the gate. Keep the engine running, ready to move at moment's notice. Move just now" Three police officers ran towards the vans.

He then grouped his police force into three. One team was asked to stay hidden, at the same spot ready to attack, in case some other terrorists showed up. Once the victims come out in the open, they were to help them, gently with at most care. If needed, they should physically carry them and board them. This is because most of them were pregnant and they may not be in a position to move fast enough to board the van quickly. The moment one van was filled they should dash out in full speed without looking back or waiting for the others.

The remaining two team, were told to take the camp from left and right side, attack the guarding solders silently one by one with utter caution without a whisper in total silence. The bomb specialist team, who came with him were asked to go on the left and right sides skirting the border of the tents and diffuse the land mines one by one again with total caution of silence. Gokul requested Jadav for one more gun and some hand grenades. Jadav now realized that Sherya was still inside the camp and is not armed. He gave Gokul two more guns, and some hand grenades. Gokul stuffed all of them in his doctor coat's pocket.

Jadav looked at him with admiration for his foresight and then he said "Gokul go inside slowly now. Walk as slow as possible as that would buy us more time. Then see that the victims are not harmed under any worst circumstances. Be very, very careful. My best wishes".

Gokul started walking inside the corridor carrying a large medicine box. For the first time he was walking inside without the gun wielding guards. As he walked slowly he strongly prayed for God's mercy for the most dangerous, dreadful operation which was going to be fought by a group of non military, non police, simple, common men and women, who had never even seen a gun in their life. The operation was the most fragile, delicate one as it involved a group of fifty-eight pregnant women, along with sixty-two nurses, and sixteen doctors, all innocent victims, whose life and death were to be decided in the coming half an hour.

Jadav and his team threw themselves on the ground and started crawling on their elbows and stomach taking cover of the dark patches. The two groups started crawling simultaneously on to both sides, on the left and right of the camp moving towards the dangerous gun wielding terrorists, guarding at the peripheral of the camp. The night was dark, without any trace of moon light, which was advantage for them, as they had laser goggles and laser guns. Jadav saw the first solder at a distance of ten meters, and from that distance he took a proper aim, and pulled his silencer gun. The man collapsed without a whimper. He crawled more about ten feet to locate the next guard. At the last minute the guard suddenly shifted and the bullet whisked past him. He became alert immediately and came charging blindly towards Jadav's direction. As he neared Jadav attacked him in a surprise move. He jumped on the guard, pinning him down, with his weight. As the hefty guard started struggling, he pressed his silencer inside him. The guard stared at him for a second, his eyes full of surprise, as the bullet pierced his body, and he collapsed in slow motion. Jadav now crawled for his next attack. Rohit, Murali and others were knocking the guards swiftly one after other, their fuming anger giving them extra power, to attack. The bomb diffusing men did their duty effortlessly as the land mines were not very complicated and their work was moving in jet speed.

Chapter 46

The raid at midnight

The crime branch police officers reached the house of the young IAS officer in the dead of the night at three AM. The house was dark and very, very silent. They surrounded the house, tiptoeing, their shoes hardly making any noise. There was no guard outside the house. Probably the IAS officer had refused the government given security. The front door was locked. With their silencer guns, they broke the front door latch, and entered softly, with utter caution, they walked like cats, searching every room, and finally reached his bead room. The door was open, and he seemed to be in deep sleep. They tiptoed near him. Six of them stood around the cot. One officer, nudged him, with his gun and said

"Get up officer! You are under arrest" They expected him to jump from his sleep, and try to flee. But he kept sleeping quietly, without moving. One of the officers, looked for the light switch, and put it on. The room was flooded with bright light. The officer now came near his head and started "Sir, you better get up just now or….." But his talk stopped half way. The sleeping young man's pillow was soaked in blood, still oozing from his head. His right hand was on the pillow, still clutching his gun. The officer sighed and shook his head. He called all his men, inside and asked them to search, everything in his house, and collect files and evidences. He came to the office room. Two long candles were still burning on the stand, placed in front of the large framed picture of Jesus Christ on the cross. The duty officer was a bit disappointed, that he could not catch the officer alive. He started looking around. His eyes fell on a thick sealed cover kept ready on the table, with a paper weight on it. He picked it up. The name "Mr. Sukvir Singh" was written on it.

After collecting all files, hard ware of his computers etc they went back to their office. Inspector General Sukvir Singh was waiting there with the other three IAS officer and Shankar. Singh took the letter and opened. He started reading loudly, for the benefit of every one seated. The letter said,

> Sir,
>
>   I start this letter with a million apologies to you all officers, my country, and the countless simple common man of our country whom I cheated. When you read this letter I won't be there. I am not ending my life, for the fear of arrest, but the guilt in my heart has become too unbearable, and I cannot wait till the long procedure of law hangs me.
>
>   Sir, when I was just five year old there was a big riot in Lucknow, where my house was torched. I was out side, and I saw my parents trapped, inside the house, screaming for help. At that time God send Gaffar Baba lifted me and ran with me to a safe place. I was given to a Muslim family where I was brought up, with all the kindness, and I was given schooling first, and then the college. I was over whelmed, with the kindness Baba showed me in every part of my life. I passed IAS and joined the Indian Administration department. I received the great guidance, from loyal people like Mr. Shankaran and others. Then after twenty five years, Baba came back into my life. He called me and asked for a favour. He wanted a job for two of his computer professionals. Just as Baba had helped me, he had helped for the schooling, of so many orphan children, not Muslims but Hindus. Since the people, he brought were properly qualified, I helped them with the employment. After some time he asked for some more favour. He said his three men needed visa. He said that they had escaped from Pakistan as there was threat for their life. This time I was not very happy to do that. But the gratitude of Baba's help weighed heavily on me and I got it done. It was five months later that I learnt that the people I had helped with employment, were professional hackers, and had rigged deep into our system. They had employed more people in different levels. They were now printing letter heads of ministers, getting signatures, faking passports and Visas, for many terrorists. When I met Baba, and asked him, he calmly said that it was the only reason, for which

he had saved my life. He also told me if I don't go with the flow, he will arrange bomb blast, in schools and hospitals. I was totally up to the neck, deep in the quicksand. It was just one month back that I learnt that they had set up a terrorist camp somewhere in Karnataka. Two days back Baba called me asked for 68 passports and said that they had selected a new spot in Lucknow, to start another terrorist camp. Then I decided this should end.

If I give the name of all the members involved and even if crime branch arrest them, the case would drag on for years. They would come out in bail, or escape from jail, or even, would continue their business, from the jail and the terrorists, would continue their operation. So I decided to end this quickly all by myself, as I am responsible and had important part in it. So I called all the members of the group for a meeting, in the pretext of payment, and bombed the entire group with the building. I personally shot Baba and his man Khan.

Sir, if it is not for the sweet dreams by which people like Baba and others, lure the millions of children, orphaned like me, in so many riots and calamities, and if the society, could take a humanitarian, kind attitudes for the future of these innocent lives, many criminals like me would not be born in future.

Apologizing deeply for my crime once again,

Yours
(I cannot say truly)
Augustus

As he was nearing the end, his voice choked. All the officers who were listening sat very still unable to control their eyes welling with tears.

After few seconds Shankar said "I am still feeling sorry for my boy. The riots are created by some political parties for their interest. But the one, who lose out on this is, the orphaned, helpless children. Why can't more people of our society, come forward, and adopt them?"

Singh cleared his throat and said "Everyone thinks, it is the responsibility, of the government, to take care of these children. But one single question always plagues me! These so called big Heroes of film world, who scream from the roof top that they are Indians, and boast about 40 and 50 core club don't they have any responsibility towards the poor men? Every rupee they have earned is from the poor man's blood. They gloat over their wealth, but what are they doing to the society? If every cine star, adopts at least 100 children there won't be any child on the road and new criminals will not be born in future. There was silence in the room as no one could answer this question!

Chapter 47

The escape

Gokul covered the long corridor walking leisurely and reached the tin door. Holding the medicine box in both hands he kicked the door open, and leaving it open, entered the hall. The uniformed nurses were waiting anxiously for the medicine. He shouted in a loud voice "Medicine arrived. You nurses keep all the patients ready for injection"

The nurses under stood the code word, and immediately put all the patients on the wheel chair. They pulled the wheel chair with the patient out of the cubicle and stood there ready to bolt. In front of every cubicle there were two patients in the wheel chairs in a ready position.

The military uniformed nurse peeped behind Gokul and asked "Where are the solders?"

He said with indifference "Madam, you have ordered piles and piles of medicine and they had to be unloaded. You agree? They are just now doing it. They are unloading the mountain of medicine boxes from the ambulance"

Before leaving the hospital for the purchase of medicine itself, Gokul had told the military nurse to give doctor's coat for three nurses for sterile condition for handling the injection. So Sherya, the baby nurse, Sona were wearing the white doctor coat.

Gokul looked at Sherya and said, "Ammu, you come here and hold the box. Let me take out the most important injection first" Ammu came near him very close and took the box in a slow motion. Gokul slipped his hands under the box, and put the gun and hand grenades into her pocket. Once it was done, he turned and looking at Baby nurse, shouted "Why are you still hanging around here? Go and call other doctors for injecting medicine" The six other doctors, by this time heard Gokul's voice, and came fast to the medicine box.

In the tent that belonged to the DNA scientist the code was already given. One of them was waiting at the door and heard Gokul's voice. They got the

141

clue to begin their operation. Urgently, they pulled some files and papers and started a fire. They threw some solutions inside so that there were mild explosion, one after another. Four doctors hid themselves behind the curtain just at the entrance of the tent, while some of them came out and screamed "Fire, There is a fire, Help" A guard nearby came running, and asked "Where, where? "The doctors pointed inside.

He ran out and picked up a fire extinguisher placed outside, and rushed in. When he crossed into the tent the doctors jumped on him and pushed him down. One took a chair and slammed it on his head. Once he was knocked off, they removed his gun and kept it as a handy weapon for further protection. They repeated the show till four of the guards fell down. Finally Tippu came rushing in. He screamed "Doctors put off the fire, save the flasks of eggs, hurry" Shouting he rushed towards the burning fire. Now all the doctors joined together, and hit him from all the side with all four guns. Even after he collapsed anger fuming into them they continued to kick and hit him.

Dr. Raju said "Wait one minute. He has to be given a special treat. After all he is our head". Tippu was hoping that Raju will give him a hand and pull him up. But Dr. Raju, opened a bottle of acid, and poured it all over him. As Tippu screamed in agony, he said "This is for insulting our Nation's pride and our Jawan's honourable uniform for your criminal activity" By this time the fire, caught up on furniture, and was becoming really dangerous. They all ran out, and entered the first tent shouting "Fire, Fire Help, Help"

Gokul and other doctors pretended to lift the medicines from the box in a slow motion. As all the doctors entered Baby and Sona, bent down and put a match stick on the cot, pre packed with the smuggled injection sprit. As huge flames leapt up, and they started shouting "Fire, sister, fire"

The military nurses were standing at the tin door, peeping out anxiously waiting for the solder. All the shouting of so many made them freeze inactive, for one second. Ammu used this commotion and climbing over the huge reception platform she shouted "Sisters all of you move out the patients immediately, run out through the door quickly take the patients away. The smoke will kill the patients, run fast"

She looked at the uniformed nurses and said "Sister let them go out of the room and wait outside till we put off the fire. Others they would suffocate and die" Even before she finished her sentence the nurses waiting for the clue, sprinted out, pushing the wheelchairs ran as fast they could. They had never gone out of the tin door since their coming and hardly knew, what lies ahead for them. But there was only a single urge, to run to escape. Within three minutes all the patients, all the six plus eleven doctors, all ran through the corridor blindly, and reached the gate by two minutes. But when they reached the gate for one moment, they were shocked to see so many uniformed guards. They were about to turn back and run. But the officers had anticipated this. Hence they ran towards the group waving their hands and shouted "We are your friends, we are police, and not terrorists. We are here to rescue you all. Please don't panic and come fast to the van" The captives still stood, confused. Knowing the urgency of time the officers moved fast, and reached them. They immediately started lifting the pregnant women bodily. The captives were now relieved of their doubts. The pregnant ladies were boarded first in the van. The nurses started helping fast and got them out of their chair. Not only the officers but even all the doctors lifted the helpless, girls and ran with them to the van, for boarding. The first van was filled and as per instruction it started out in full speed and went away without waiting. The doctors and nurses got into the second van and it followed the first van. The vehicles rushed through the long cave, and then through the open gate, kept open by Jadav. Then they started climbing down the hills through rough narrow road. Officers waiting at the bottom of the road spotted the vans coming down and broke into cheers and clapping. All the vans reached them and stopped.

The victims were too dazed and still sat in the van. All the pregnant ladies and nurses were rushed to the nearest airport where a special military aeroplane waited for them. They were boarded, and by one hour, they landed, in a newly constructed military airport in Panvel. From there, they were quickly transported to the waiting hospital. Once they were handed over to the doctors and nurses the officers heaved a sigh of relief.

The eleven research doctors and six others were taken to a hotel at the nearby place. They were examined by doctors. They started treating them for a post panic and trauma situation and were told to rest, for three days before they could go back to their home. The first thing they all did was to call, their near and dear one of the family. They were already cautioned, not to mention anything about the real event. So they informed their families that that the project was over and they would return home in two day. Ananya's father, retired colonel Rao, was that happiest man, to hear in son in law's voice. As he closed the line, his lips murmured a silent prayer thanking God for his kindness.

Chapter 48

The war begins

Once all the patients, nurses and doctors disappeared down the corridor, Gokul and Sherya heaved a sigh of relief. Sona and Baby, who were pretending to put out the fire near the cot, along with Gokul and Sherya were the only person left in the room. The uniformed nurses were still looking down the corridor, their eye scanning, for their soldiers who were suppose to bring the medicines. When five minutes had passed, and still there was no sign of guards, she turned to Gokul and yelled "Doctor! Where are my solders? Why they are taking this much time?"

Gokul just surged his shoulders and shook his head with a straight face. The fire on the cot was created by alcohol. Because of its low ignition temperature, the bed sheets of the cot did not catch fire and the fire started dyeing down. While Sona started wondering whether she should start another fire, one of the uniformed nurse turned in her direction. She saw that the fire is douched. She said with relief "Thank God! The fire is gone and there is no more smoke. We can get the patients back."

The other military nurse stepped into the corridor to call the patient back. She was shocked to see the empty corridor starring back at her. Till the last point where the corridor ended there was no trace of a single human soul to be seen.

She burst out screaming madly at the top of her voice "Doctor, Where did you ask the patients to wait? They had to be waiting just here, at the outside But they are not here"

Gokul, looked at Sherya and said "I don't know Madam. Where can they go? Oh, I think that in their fear of smoke, they could have run up to the gate, to escape from danger of choking. We will send some nurse and get them back"

He was thinking his mind racing to get an excuse so that all four of them could escape. He then decided that first he would save Sona and Baby. He and Sherya could escape by shooting down the sisters. But the fate worked differently. The uniformed one said "No need for any one of you to go. I would get them back with my soldiers"

She picked up the cell and called her solder. There was no answer. She called one after other every soldier and there was no answer from any one. The two ladies stared at each other, fear of their boss written all over their face. One of them now unexpectedly pounced on Sona and pulled her by her hair and started screaming "You are the culprit! You started the fire! And now my men are not answering my call.. Tell me the truth, who is your partner here or I will just no shoot you"

She pushed Sona down violently and started kicking her mercilessly with her boots. Gokul signalled Sherya and they were about to use their gun, when the least unexpected happened.

Jadav and his team having killed all the solders decided, to go in and check if any of the patients was still left back inside the room. He asked most of his men to wait at the gate, and only ten of them entered the room. Just as stepped in, he knew he had made a terrible mistake. There were still four persons left in the room and one sister was being beaten cruelly. There were now four gun holding lady nurses surrounded Sona with their gun pointed at her.

On the spur of the moment he thought of a plan, to play it safe, try to buy time, by pretending to be a terrorist solders. Pulling his cap down on his face hiding it partially, he said "Madam, we all have come now. Leave this lady to us, and we would teach her a good lesson" Saying he moved close to Sona.

The angry lady stopped hitting and turned to Jadav and shouted "Where were you all this much time? Were you all dead or what? Why did you take so much time to come in? Why was your phone not working? And where the hell is the medicine?" And where are the patients?"

Jadav looked from Sona to Baby and signaled with his eyes- a very minute wink. He then turned to the uniform and said, "Madam there seems to be some problem with the net work and hence we did not hear your call at all". Now he looked at Sona and shouted in an authoritative voice "Why are you two stupid nurses still standing here and looking at out face? Don't you have any brain? Both of you run out fast and get back all the patients waiting outside near the gate. Hurry, and be very quick" Though Sona and Baby did not know Jadav was their savvier, they still took the opportunity and ran out for their lives all the way through the corridor till they reached the gate.

Jadav now looked at Gokul and Sherya and said, "Why you two are waiting here, you also go and help, to get the patients back"

But before they could move the nurse said "Why should they go now? Already two nurses had gone. And where are the medicines? You are yet to answer that question?"

Jadav not having prepared for this question became tongue tied for fraction of a second and started "Oh, the medicines. Madam the solders could not bring them immediately as the patients crowded around them blocking their way ....." He had not completed his sentence. But the uniformed nurse now stepped closer very near him and was about to say something, when her eyes fell on Jadav's cap. She stood shocked for one moment and then started yelling

"Hey, these are not our solders, they are outsiders!!" Catch them immediately" Instantly the three nurses wielding guns surrounded them and screamed "Who are you? First all of you put down your guns immediately go down on your knees and or I would shoot these two the Doctor and nurse" Now two soldiers appeared from nowhere and each one of them had a gun pointed on Gokul and Sherya. Jadav looked at the tough terrorists. If he opened the fire, definitely they would shoot Sherya and Gokul.

Suddenly half a dozen solders, wielding machine guns, appeared on the platform, from nowhere. Jadav and his team, decided to play it along, and dropped their guns and went down on their knees. He was shocked to see so many solders appearing and so suddenly. As he looked at their cap he noticed green florescent band on their caps. He now understood that the lack of that band, in their cap of their uniform was the one which made the nurses spot them.

He looked at Gokul and Sherya. They two were pretending to be dump and acting frightened and nervous with all these events. Sherya had leant that playing dump is the best thing to do for now. That way the solders would not pay much attention to them.

The terrorist nurse started questioning Jadav "Are you a real army person from the army? How did you find out about us? How did you get inside our cell? Tell me all the truth or I would smash your head"

Jadav looked at her with unflinching eyes and said "You terrorist thought you are all very smart. But our army is smarter. See how easily we cracked your den door in no time and entered"

The nurse hissed between he clenched teeth "But you are not going back alive from here and let me see what your army is going to do......"

As she was talking, the two nurses standing near her buckled and collapsed one after other. Gokul and Sherya shot them through their pockets with their hidden silencer gun and continued to stand dump. As the nurse's attention was momentarily diverted in a flash, Jadav and his men grabbed their automatic rifles and all the nurses and all the solders collapsed within a second.

But before they could even breathe, more and more solders kept appearing and the battle raged on and on. It seemed that the Jadav and his team, could not win as the solders now distinctly outnumbered them, and more and more of them kept on appearing on the platform.

No one except Jadav knew that it was Sherya and Gokul who had fired the first shot knocking the nurses and helped Jadav's team to pick up their guns. Their guns were still in their pocket. But they did not want to shoot another time and turn the solder's attention towards them. She stood thinking feverishly as she watched the rain of bullet from both side.

Sherya cursed herself for the enormous, unpardonable failure of herself. For so many days she was in the camp and she knew there were solders all around. But never once it occurred to her to find out the den of these men where did they keep all their ammunition! She should have noticed that all over the hospital there were only patients, nurses and doctors. There was no tent for the soldiers! And in the past, on so many occasions she had wondered about the need of the most stupid looking, useless, huge platform on which, the reception desk stood. Now she saw that this platform was now open behind the C- shaped reception. All the soldiers were coming out of it like ants, in tens and twenties. As a heap of solders fell for the powerful guns of Jadav and troop, more solders came out. Sherya knew that with all the power of Jadav and team, they would not be able to fight an entire army of terrorists and soon will run out of their ammunition.

She looked at Gokul and gestured to him. Looking still stupid they started, moving to their sides like crabs inch by inch so that their movements were not visible. They moved till they reached the inner most of side of the room near the wall. They were now standing perpendicular to the fighting line and had reached the back of the reception desk. They could now see the open door of the well of the underground room, from where the soldiers were climbing out. They looked at each other and nodded. Then simultaneously they picked up four hand grenade each holding two, and bit of the pins. Using all their force, they threw them inside, the well at the same time. She shouted at the same time, **"Jadav Sir run, all of you run fast, and get out of this place"** Though Jadav and his team did not understand what she meant, still his troop started backing through the door very fast, keeping the firing still on.

For one fleeting second, the terrorists felt glee on gaining an upper hand, and jumped from the platform to chase the withdrawing enemy. But before that could jump, a thundering blast blew up the entire desk of the platform on to the ceiling. Instantly the soldiers were blown into pieces and their scattered dead bodies flew in all direction. Jadav's team which had moved a few paces now wondered as to what had caused the explosion. The very moment they had thrown the grenades, Gokul tightly held Shery's hand and started running dragging her in full speed. But the explosion started instantly. The room was too long and the explosion was too strong! Since the solders had stored all their ammunition inside the well, the explosion became a continuous chain of explosions. It rained fire, and huge burning chips of wood and other materials, flew in all direction. Gokul and Sherya ran very fast through falling, burning wood, but were repeatedly hit. Finally both of them collapsed even before reaching the tin door. Jadav and his team waited in the corridor for a second, hearing the blast.

But ones Jadav realized that the blasts are not just a single one, but a chain of blasts and was not going to stop, he shouted "Sherya and Gokul! Come out fast" There was no response. He turned to his team and yelled, "They had not come out!" He turned back immediately, and ran inside in jet speed. He kept shouting repeatedly, "Sherya, Sherya, Where are you" Rohit, Murali and all of them ran back with him.

The room was filled with dense smoke and nothing was visible. The carbon monoxide, sulphur di- oxide and other poisonous gases from the burning ammunition choked their breath, and they coughed miserably. Determined in their pursuit all of them crawled on their knees and blindly searched with their hands. Burning fire balls, continued to fall on them, and many of them were severely injured. Still they continued searching, spreading their hands in darkness, and trying to feel their team mates. By this time all the curtains and furniture caught fire and the fire raged on becoming more and more fierce. Jadav felt Sherya's shoulder and shouted, "She is here, lift her" As others helped to lift her they also found Gokul. They all ran out for the second time. In spite of his wounds Jadav insisted, on carrying the unconscious Sherya and Rohit carried Gokul. They ran with all their might through the raging fire. The team which was waiting at the gate had brought out more van, that one of the terrorists, for extra space. Jadav's team was all badly wounded and all of them were bleeding. All of got into the two vans, and vans raced out as now the entire camp, up to the front gate had caught fire. There were continuous blasts as the ammunition stored hidden in different parts of the camp caught fire. They just reached the cave door, when, the entire cave started caving in, due to the impact of blasts. They just made it out, when the whole cave collapsed and became a heap of stones.

As they reached the bottom, they were all rushed to the hospital. Jadav had two bullets on his left hands and wounds all over his body causing a lot of bleeding. All his brave team had at least one or two bullets, and was severely injured. Sherya and Gokul's condition was very bad. The burning chips of wood etc had got deeply lodged all over their body. Besides this they had suffered suffocation for a short time. The doctors said that it will be a very long time before they could get up.

Chapter 49

The recovery

Back at the temporary hospital in Panvel things were happening fast. The sixth floor was converted into a large conference hall. 62 recliner chairs were arranged in rows. Facing the chairs, a podium was created, equipped with the mike, computer, projector etc. A large white screen for the projector was placed on the wall, facing the chairs. Dr Neel Mukerji, a world famous physiatrist and hypnotist, who flew from New York, for the special mission, landed, in the special military air port, at Panval. A team of senior doctors received him in the airport, and on reaching the hospital, briefed him about the case of all the patients. Then they took him to the conference room, and showed him the arrangement. He was satisfied with the arrangement and he gave further instruction, to the nurses, which had to be done, as preparation for the secession. The next day at nine thirty AM all the 62 girls were brought into the hall, and were seated, in the recliner chairs. They were injected with a sedative injection. The hall had a mild lighting, where a soft relaxing music played on, at the background. Some aroma candles, kept the hall filled with fresh fragrance. Dr Neel entered the room and took his position on the platform. Other doctors and nurses sat, in row, on the side of the podium. The technicians, who had to operate the mike and computers, took their seats on the side of the screen.

Dr Neel started his speech.-

"Dear friends, in a most unfortunate, unexpected event, all of you young women, were subjected to a serious accident. The accident had produced deep scars in your mind, you are still in shock, and you are haunted by night mares. All of you had lost your previous, memory. This programme is, to sooth your mind and bring back your old memory, by taking you, to a tour to your past."
As he talked the lights dimmed, and the large white screen became alive. He continued in a soft velvet like, soothing voice, which hypnotized ever one. The

patients slowly sank into an altogether different world the virtual world which the doctor was showing them.

The screen showed a village now and Dr Neel continued "This is the village in Karnataka, where you all lived. See this, village cows, the well and the village school. One day, four Americans came to your village and enrolled you all for a nursing course. You all started learning, happily and went through the training" The picture showed some random, Americans, not specifically focusing on any one, and a some nurse's training courses, going on some part of the world. Because of the power of Dr Neel's voice, and effect of sedative injection the girls got totally involved and really felt that they were a part of that course, and were sitting right there, in that spot. The voice continued "One day you all were called for a special emergency service for helping victims of a train accident that occurred near Bangalore" Now the picture showed a train accident, victims caught under the train, some of them seriously bleeding, some screaming for help etc.

Dr continued, "See ladies, this is the painful site, where you all went in like God and helped them. After that you went to help for another calamity and this time it was flooding in Kashmir, the worst disaster in past years. You all served these victims. Next you went to Nepal to help the victims of an earth quake." When he talked about Kashmir and Nepal, the screen pictures was moving through the agony of the destruction in Kashmir and Nepal.

Dr. continued, "But after all these selfless service, when you were coming back, your bus met with a major accident. Your bus rolled into a deep valley half way, and remained there, hanging for six hours, till all of you were rescued." The screen now showed a bus hanging on the edge of a hill. Every one gasped at the sight of the dreadful picture. Dr. now continued, "Luckily all of you were rescued, without any major injury. But the hours of peril, hanging between life and death, left a very deep fear Psychosis, in you all. This affected your memory and you all started getting nightmares, with wild things like abduction by terrorists etc. But, here after, you would forget, all about the accident, and remember, only the nice things you did, the saving and caring of the hundreds of people for whom you were just nothing but angels". Then he further lowered his voice and almost whispered, "Now you all would go into a deep sleep, when I snap my finger" He starred counting…. "Here you go, ten, nine, eight ………. two, one"

He snapped his finger. All the patients went into a deep hypnotic sleep, just like a miracle. He talked again," Now all the bitter memories, will be erased from your memory, once for all. When you wake up you will have only happy memories" He snapped his finger again. All the patients woke up smiling.

The lights flooded the room once again. Dr. Neel walked out with the team of doctors. The patients were served, lunch in the same chair, and were asked to relax. They all went to sleep again. The light were switched off, totally except, for two zero watt blue lights. The girls had already gone, into deep hypnotic sleep again. The nurses, now flattened the recliner's position like bed, so that they could sleep comfortably.

Dr. Neel came out with other doctors. He said," We will repeat the same secession for three days. Then, all throughout their lives, these girls, cannot remember a trace, of anything, that had happened, but for what we had showed them." Doctors thanked him profusely.

Dr. Neel asked," By the way doctor, the other thing I told you, about buying some memento, souvenirs etc, from the places they had visited---. You know that would reinforce the story of their visit" Doctors said,"Yes Dr.Neel, we had already purchased mementoes from Kashmir and Nepal and had packed it all in their new bags, with new dresses etc. They would carry these new suitcases when they leave here".

As the hypnotic secession continued, back in the hospital things were happening. All the pregnant girls were operated, in groups of fifteen a day. The girls were not shown the babies, but the babies were removed, when the girls were still under the effect of anesthesia. The babies were rushed to the incubators. The girls were again, highly sedated, and given very nutritious food and vitamin injection, and well looked after. Round the clock the doctors and nurses took care of the premature babies, and by their relentless efforts, the babies started picking up health.

The girls, who all had finished secession, were feeling very happy to see the new suitcases, and all the gifts for their family members. They were taken by flight to Mysore, and from there they were taken to their village by bus. Dr. Aruna, and Panchayat members were waiting for them. There was all joy, cheer, and happiness, as the girls got united with their families.

One month after the delivery, the teen girls also started their hypnotic secession in the same way. With all the sedation and medicines, none of them even remembered, that they were once pregnant. The talk given by Dr. Neel in the same way, but only the pictures and contents differed. It was now their participation in a handicraft exhibition, held in Dubai, then in Malaysia and finally in Singapore. The picture showed, close up picture of the intricate, minute, highly skilled, handicraft materials, which they had made, and sold in the exhibition. The pictures also showed the various places, they went for site seeing. The hypnotic power was so strong and gripping, that the girls were really feeling, that were just there, standing in the exhibition, in Dubai or Singapore. The secession went for five days. Suitcases with gift items from Dubai, Malaysia and Singapore were handed over to the girls along with new dresses from the same place. Just the one day before the girls had to be moved, the senior, doctor, in charge of the project, asked the surgeons, some thing, in a deep worried voice full of concern. The Surgeon replied "Don't worry sir, as per instruction, we conducted the delivery with minimum insertion. Even that small scar, was made invisible, by grafting, by our plastic surgeons. All these girls could marry in future life, and lead, a happy, normal life. No one, not even any doctor, could identify that they were pregnant once." The senior said, "Thank God for his mercy" Next day just like the previous case, these 58 girls were moved to their villages, with handful of gifts, and a sweet memory of their trip.

After one more months the babies came out of incubators, all 122 of them, were healthy, bouncy babies. Cars came in the darkness of night, one after other secret papers were signed, and sealed. By three days, all the babies were gone. After two more days the make shift hospital was dismantled and the final work of converting it into a five star hotel began.

Chapter 50

Dr. Bhaskar reveals

After initial treatment all the officers were shifted to Mumbai. Jadav and his team were out of hospital in five weeks. He went to Sherya's hospital to see her. She and Gokul were in nearby rooms. They had removed one bullet, and hundreds of tiny splinters from her body. But she was still too weak, and was kept under sedation to bear the pain. She was sleeping when Jadav visited her. He stood there, very still, looking at her pale face, for a long time. Then he went to Gokul's room. His condition was still worse. As he tried to cover Sherya with his body, from the splinters, he had more splinters on his back side. They were all removed. But he was compelled, all the time to sleep on his stomach. He was now sleeping.

Jadav joined duty. After two days a meeting was called on. Commissioner Gadre, Jadav and all the eleven Scientists were called to attend the meeting. Mr. Gadre said "Since you all have picked up health, and our officer Jadav, is also here we want to know the answers for so may un answered questions. To begin with why did they abduct research doctors like you? Why did they first select the young girls, aspiring to be models or singers, and what they did with them? Then why were they killed? Why were all the girls, so young lifted from the village? How did they get them pregnant? What were the terrorist planning to do, with so many babies? We can understand luring young youths and making them terrorists. But, these tiny babies, how they are going to be of any help for them? I want to hear all the truth, without a single omission"

Dr. Bhaskar Raju started talking. He said, "Sir, me and my team and all those young girls would be indebted throughout our life for all your men, for rescuing us from those dreadful terrorists. We never dreamed that we would be alive an see the outside world again. Especially thanks to that young, brave lady, officer who risked her life for saving our life.

To begin with once we reached the camp we were told to fuse the donor eggs and donor sperm in sterile condition which can be later implanted. But once the eggs were fertilized they asked us to go for DNA modification. We have to identify the genes which can cause potential diseases like cancer, kidney or liver failure or even HIV, and remove them from the fertilized egg, so that baby born would never be affected by these ailments. They also asked us to develop such immune system in these babies so that any epidemics like malaria, dengue, which would be around, will not affect them. These babies are also to be provided with some specials genes, which would make healing, of any major wound, very fast, and they would bleed very less if there is an accident"

Mr. Gadre said "Is this all really possible by a gene alteration?"

Dr.Raju smiled and said "Sir, a very long research for many years are needed to find a said gene and then again years of research is to be carried of, to do even a small alteration or blocking of a gene. In a short time, since our landing, we knew that these people did not have much knowledge of genes, and we played along their way, and said we had really done those alteration. But honestly we did remove some genetic disorders from the fertilized eggs so that the babies born would not suffer from those diseases. We also added some known genes so that the babies would have a higher immunity. Now all the generation arising out of these babies would carry forward these healthy traits.

We came to know only latter, that they had kidnapped very young girls of fifteen and sixteen and got them impregnated with the fertilized eggs. With utter cruelty they made the girls pregnant with twins or triplets. They thought that the very young unmarried village girls would have much physical strength to go through the pregnancies. But in reality these girls, were too young, for the pregnancy as their uterus were not fully strengthened. Above all the twins and triplets pregnancy, lead all of them into medical complications. Hence most of them had to be kept at bed rest, with monitors and this proved very costly for the terrorists.

Now the terrorists started getting more wild ideas and wanted to fuse human cells with some animal cells so that the terrorist would be born cruel, tough and very strong. We destroyed all these eggs and cell given to us. We nodded for everything they said, and in the time we got, we made genuine research of identifying some serious ailments and copied all our data in secret tiny plastic cells and kept them hidden with us all the time"

Gadre said, "Still you are yet to tell us tell us what they did to those young girls and why they killed them?

Dr Raju said, "The terrorists wanted to produce a generation of future terrorists who cannot be easily identified. Since the terrorists face structures are almost known all over the world, they thought of this idea. First they befriended gullible girls. They created stomach cramps by feeding them with medicated chocolates. Then their agent took them to the terrorist camp doctor, and in the pretext of treating their cyst, they fooled these girls and treated them with hormone pills to produce a multiple number of eggs, which could have even killed them. After extracting the eggs, they murdered them, because they were potential witness to their crime. If these girls had gone to any doctor, they would come to know about the truth, and they also knew the place where it was done. That was the reason behind murdering them immediately. The reason they specifically picked up these girls, was that they were not only good looking, but were blessed with the talent of music or dance, and also lived all alone. That way there was no danger of any immediate uproar, or investigation, about the dead one. Their agents also collected the bodies, and cremated them, as an eye wash for the police sake. They had the girls addresses and just kept the family fooled by sending money or e mail etc for four months

According to their plan, now the terrorists would have a generation of different faces, good looking, and talented men. After the babies are born they were planning to use one fourth of these children for terror attacks and the remaining would form the solders of their terrorism." Gadre said, "Most of these were done without your knowledge. Then how did you find out the details of their operation?"

Raju continued "The terrorists used to provide us, with drinks as a special bonus. We found out that Tippu had a weakness for drinks and most night he use come to check our work, in a drunken condition. We used this weakness. We saved all the bottles provided for us, and supplied him, with more and more drinks and talked with him. It was in this drunken state, that he gave away most of their secrets. Bur however we tried, we were not able to get an answer from him as what was the secret entrance. Of course even if we had got it, we could not have escaped, as they would have shot us down as they shot a nurse, and three doctors, who helped them with implanting the girls.

Gadre and Jadav sat shell shocked, tongue tied, on hearing such a horror story. Gadre cleared his throat, and continued, "Tell me doctor what were they going to do with these one fourth, that is about thirty babies? What type of terror attack could be done, with these tiny babies who cannot even walk?"

Dr. Raju sat silent for some time. Then he whispered in a low voice, "These terrorists had obtained some special hormone injection, from China. They would inject the new born babies, with these injection every day. Because of this high dose of hormones the babies would start growing in enormous speed. By the age of three, they would look like ten years old and would also have that mental growth. These children by that time, would been trained in music and acting. Thus in three years, these babies would now be boys would enter the glamour world. They would start to give live performances. We know the craze of our population for this glamour world. For each performances, millions would gather for listening. Then......"

His voice choking, he stopped for some time. Then in a stammering voice, he told about, the most horrid, convoluted, blood curling, cruelest attack ever imagined, planned by the terrorist. As he finished, Gadre and Jadav had to stop and remember to breath. Their hearts burnt with fury thinking about the unmitigated destruction that could have occurred, but for their timely attack of the camp. That too ...just by a chance anonymous note. There was a total dead silence in the room as each shot up a prayer to the Lord who had saved them.

Later the doctors were profusely thanked for their help. They were all told to sign a document of undertaking that they would never reveal, any time in their life, to any one, about the event. Then they were allowed to go home.

Gasdre asked Jadav about the babies' adoption.

Jadav said "Of the 122 babies, 5 were girls and all other were boys. We gave all, but three boys, to the military and police officers, who already had grown up children, and who were happy to help for adoption. Sir, you remember the three boys, who were killed in the trekking expedition near Chikmanglore? We called those three parents, and told them that their boys have died in an accident, but the police came to know only now. We told them that there were some orphan boys for adoption, and they wish they can adopt them. The Poor parents! They considered it God's wish that they adopted the boys. We called the four parents of the girls who were murdered, and told them in mild words that their daughters were killed in accidents, and their bodies were disposed off by police, as the identity could not be established. But if they were willing, they can adopt, four orphaned girls, and give them home. They took the girls happily. It is possible that those baby girls might possess the genes of their daughter."

Gadre got up and patted Jadav and said, "Milind, You had handled everything excellently well. I am proud of you" Then after some discussion he said, "Jadav, I think we should request the government, to make some changes. Taking a serious view of the lapses in various levels government, they should take some serious decision. When any foreigner enters India, police had to keep an eye on their visa, and deport them if they try to over stay. The department of forest should, employ special officers, with the responsibility to periodically check, the hills and caves, mountains. Jadav said, "Sir, a number of people infiltrate our country, through Bangladesh and Nepal. These people have no identity of any sort, form the migration population, and most of them get employed as unskilled manual labourers,. When crime is committed, we have no way of checking on them. Government should make it obligatory to make working permit for all these migrating people, completed with their fingerprints. Though it is huge task, once their finger prints are on record, any one will hesitate before a crime" Gadre started laughing saying, "All these would be only on our wild imagination" and Jadav joined in his laughter.

Chapter 51

The truth

Three months flew away. After all treatment and some plastic surgery, to cover the burn injuries, Sherya joined back to duty. Jadav telephoned her and in the evening he dropped at her house to meet her. He came with a large bunch of flowers. Sherya opened the door and said "Good evening Sir, please come in" Her face was all surprise when Jadav, the iron man, gave her the flowers. He said, "Welcome back to office!"

He took the chair across her in the small coffee table of her house. They generally talked about every thing which took place when she was in hospital. She asked with a wicked glint in her eyes "Sir, Why you had given away only four baby girls? Why you had still kept back one baby girl? Are you going to adopt it by any chance?" Jadav looked at the suppressed smile in her eyes and said "I wish I was able to do it. May be in future I would do it some time. But now there was another person very badly need of the baby. When I met Gokul in hospital and had a long conversation with him I learnt from Dr. Gokul, that he was married for past nine years, and still has no children so for. His wife is at present in USA and he told us not to inform her, about the accident. She would be coming back by two days. Gokul was discharged one week ago. I met him before discharge, and told him that I wanted to present, the baby girl, to him as bonus, for what all he did for us. He was too thrilled and happy"

Sherya smiled happily and her voice softening with the memory of Gokul's help, she said "He is such a good man. But for his intelligent plan, of the girls falling sick, we could not rescued the captives"

Suddenly remembering, something, she said, "Sir, over the telephone you told me, all about the plan of the terrorist. But you did not tell me one thing about the attack, they were planning, with the forty tiny babies?"

Jadav looked away for a moment and said, "Sherya, why you have to hear that? Everything has ended good. So don't worry about that plan. I think I should leave now" He started getting up.

Sherya said, "No sir, you cannot leave, without telling me. I insist Sir, remember, I was a part of the entire operation. You have to tell me" Jadav said, "Ok it was like this." He was silent again, for few second, and then started talking very, very softly, almost whispering. Sherya, placed both her hands, on the table, and leaned forward, trying her best to listen. In five seconds, Jadav finished his talk. Sherya sat frozen. Her eyes stared, with a vacant look, too traumatized, too stunned unable to breath or talk. Jadav watched her for a second and called her, "Sherya," His voice brought her, to the world of reality, and suddenly, she burst into tears, crying, weeping with all her heart, helplessly, her body shaking with tremors. Jadav watched her, for some time silently. Then he got up and walked around the table, and came near her chair.

He gently held her shoulder and said, "Sherya, please, don't cry. It is all over now! And you are the one and only one, who single handed, prevented all this. Then why should you cry?" Sherya's sobs stopped slowly. She wiped her face. Jadav was still standing there. Then he said in a hesitant voice "Sherya, Actually I was thinking, of asking you something. But now, I think it is not the proper time. I better leave and I will come back some other time"

Sherya suddenly realised, that she was sitting in the chair, when he, her boss, was standing. She, hurriedly pushed her chair back, and got up urgently, and said, "No, No Sir, I am fine now. Please ask me, whatever you want to ask" Jadav looked at her eyes steadily for one moment, then hesitated, and looked away. Sherya became impatient and said, "Yes Sir, please, go ahead and ask, I am waiting"

Jadav said "Sherya will you please marry me?"

On hearing these words, from Jadav the tough guy, Sherya just stared at him. He had been her idol for years. She couldn't believe her ears for one second. She knew Jadav had a hard time communicating anything other than orders. Then with a mischievous smile she said, "OK Jadav Sir. We have worked together for five years. I can have many reasons to marry you. But please tell me, at least one good reason, why?"

Jadav looked at her for one moment, steadily, and then he looked very puzzled, and then, suddenly hugged her in a tight embrace. He whispered in her ears, "There are not many reasons. But there is one, and only one, good reason. If terrorists attack my house, I would have a brave wife who will save me even from the deepest mountains." Sherya burst into uncontrolled laughter and Jadav joined her in laughing.

It was ten in the night and as usual, commissioner Gadre went to bed. Every day night, the secret what Dr. Bhaskar Raju had told two months back in a stammering choking voice echoed in his ear again?

> *"Prior to one of those performances, these children, would have been injected, with a lethal virus strain. Half through, their performance, they would start coughing, and collapse and die. In a fraction of a second, the dreadful, strong virus, produced by the cough, would spread like fire among the audience, and every one would collapse, and die coughing. This virus would spread further and further in the air, and keep on affecting, more and more people. Thus millions of people, our entire country of Indians would be wiped off in just two days with this ghastly plan".*

Gadre prayed the same frevent prayer, which he prayed every day. "Oh God, Please, Clear the veil of evils from the terrorists minds, and make them human. Bless them, with all your kindness, to understand the value of human life."

END

Printed in the United States
By Bookmasters